DANCE FOR ME

ALDER ACADEMY BOOK 1

ERIN TREJO

CONTENTS

1
———

WHISPER

"I don't understand what any of this means," I say rubbing at my temples. This is all a headache. Everything in my life has been a headache. Day after day, year after year.

"It means that they have decided to take you in while you're in college. This is amazing news, Whisper." I stare at her. Really look at her. My caseworker. She isn't your typical looking caseworker, not like the ones I've had in the past. She's taller, more poised, but she has the personality of a street kid which is why I get along with her so well. She's treated me with respect over the last four years and for that I'm grateful.

"Why would some family decide to take an eighteen-year-old girl in? I haven't been adopted before now," I say rolling my eyes. Asia sits forward, resting her elbows on her knees as she glares at me.

"Maybe they're nice people?" she says.

"Or maybe they're psychotic killers. Human traffickers. Hell, maybe they are going to cut me up and eat me," I say sitting back in my chair. Neither of us speak for a long second before she bursts into laughter.

"Eat you? Really? I'd be more afraid for them, Whisper. This is your chance to go to college, have a shot at a real family. The Remington's are wealthy and have stability. They are offering you the chance to further your education. You're going."

"Technically, I am eighteen and don't have to follow these rules," I add raising an eyebrow.

"If you didn't get into so much trouble, that might be true, but you Miss Whisper are hell on earth. Which means the judge already signed off on all of this," she says with a smirk. One I'd like to slap off her face. I don't like being told what to do. In fact, I don't do well with authority at all.

"This is bullshit."

"Maybe, but I see it as a chance for you to make something out of your life. Besides, I hear Alder Academy has an amazing dance program."

"Considering I sing, that won't do me any good," I snap back. She raises her eyebrow and shakes her head.

"Considering I have seen you dance; I think you're full of shit." This is why I like her. She challenges me even when she shouldn't. She makes me feel like there is something out there for me even when I don't see it myself. Hell, I don't believe there is anything in this life that I can do right.

"This is stupid," I say once more.

"Too bad. It can be stupid all you want it to be but you're going." She shoves out of the chair and walks toward the door as I watch her. This is it. The last time I have to see her. Alder Academy? I've looked it up. All it is, is a bunch of entitled spoiled rich fucks. Not where I want to be, and it sure as hell isn't somewhere I plan to stay. I won't fit in there just like I don't fit in anywhere. I watch the back of Asia's head as she heads out the door before flipping her off. Fuck her. With a sigh, I stand from the bed and grab my bag before following the way she went out. I'm down the stairs of my current girls' home when I see the couple standing outside with smiles on their overly perfect faces. She's gorgeous, could pass as a supermodel. He isn't bad himself.

Stepping outside, everyone's eyes come to meet mine. She steps forward first, holding her hand out.

"I'm Debra. It's so nice to meet you," she says pleasantly. I'm not completely rude so I step forward and take her hand.

"Whisper."

"I love that name. It's one I've never heard before. So unique."

"It's stupid," I inform her, pulling my hand back and letting my arm fall to my side.

"Well, I think it's beautiful."

"You would," I grumble.

"Whisper! Your manners," Asia reminds me.

"Sorry," I say sweetly batting my lashes at Debra. She isn't going to be able to handle me. This isn't going to work.

"Well, I'm Nathan. It's nice to meet you as well and if you don't like your name, what would you like to be called?" Jesus, even his voice is as pleasant as Debra's. I roll my eyes and shake my head, my long dark hair falling over my shoulder.

"Whisper. Just like everyone else calls me. Are we going?" Nathan doesn't look shocked at my outburst as he nods his head and holds his hand out for my bags. Shaking my head, I walk to the trunk of his SUV and toss them in before slamming it closed. Asia grabs my arm and pulls me against her.

"Be nice, Whisper. They seem great."

"She's a pushover."

"Don't push her then," she says with a smile. A fake front for the fake parents.

"Fine." I'll say anything to get her off my ass right now. I want to get the hell out of here and get on with this bullshit of a life. Stepping away from Asia, I climb into the back of the SUV and slam the door closed. Debra and Nathan share a smile before climbing in.

I watch out the window as a part of my life passes by. A past that I hate. A past that I love. A past that made me who I am. I'm not sure who this new Whisper will be once I settle in and make myself a place at Alder Academy. Something tells me that I will still be me. Just which version?

2

STEELE

"You see Tricia today?" Knox, one of my brothers asks as we walk the long hallway.

"Don't I see her every day?" He chuckles when Callan, our other brother steps up next to us.

"What are we talking about?"

"Tricia and how good her ass looks in those little shorts she had on," Knox states. I roll my eyes as we make our way into the coach's office. His eyes come up to see it's the three of us before he drops what he's doing.

"You three. Why the hell can't you just stay out of trouble?" he snaps, resting his hands on his hips.

"What trouble?" I ask tilting my head to the side with my signature smirk on my face. We're known for trouble. Around here we're known as the Triple A's. This is our school. We run it, we own it. Nothing happens in this town without our knowledge. We are the fucking Alder's.

"Really, Steele? Do I need to remind your asses that even though you run the world in these parts, you still have to put in some kind of effort?" I love when he gets all pissed off like this. It makes me hard.

"Need I remind you that I don't give two shits about any of this?"

"Not even football?" He would pull that card. Alder Academy is number one in college football. That's because my brothers and I are top fucking athletes. Without us, this team would fall to shit. We keep it running.

"Don't pull the football card, Ray," Knox chimes in.

"I have to or you three don't listen. Your dad's been up my ass about your grades." I see the look in his eyes, and I know that it's hard for him to deal with us and the football team. Dad is always off on business and leaves Ray to pick up the pieces. Ray is like a father figure to the three of us but that doesn't mean that we don't give him hell.

"Why? Who's failing now?" I ask glancing over at Callan. He's the youngest of the three of us.

"Fuck off, Steele," he grumbles.

"Get your shit together, Cal! We don't need him breathing down our backs," I growl turning to face my brother, Cal.

"It's not just his grades, Steele. You boys are stirring up shit with your undercover searching that isn't as secretive as you think it is," Ray tells me.

"What the hell is that supposed to mean?" Now my anger is directed back at him.

"It means your dad knows you're looking into the shit with the Macron family history." That has us all stopping in our tracks.

"What's he care?" Knox asks stepping closer to the desk. Ray looks around making sure no one is within hearing distance before he walks around the desk crossing his arms over his chest.

"You know why he cares. There's a reason that those things

are kept secret, Steele." He always directs shit at me since I'm the oldest.

"And? If he wants us to handle things accordingly, we need to know these things. It would be a shit ton easier if he would just tell us," I remind him.

"Well, tonight might be your chance. He's on his way back to Rolling Springs."

"What for?" Callan asks standing up straighter. We all know that when Dad comes around, shit usually gets bad and involves us.

"Don't know, don't care. He said he wants to see you all at the house at seven after practice." Knox huffs out a breath that I understand all too well. No one is in the mood to deal with our dad tonight. We have games coming up and need to practice.

"I'll think about it," I say, turning and heading toward the door.

"Don't you dare think about it. Show your ass up, Steele!" Flipping him off over my shoulder, I step back into the hallway with my brothers right behind me.

"What do you think this shit is?"

"How the hell do I know. Why don't you get your shit together and get your grades up before it's all of our asses on the line, Callan!" My father has made it very clear that we are all to graduate college here with a degree in business. The problem is, none of us really give a shit about the business. We like the dark side of things, the back side that not many know about. We like getting our hands dirty. I don't see myself ever working in an office the way my father does. Callan maybe, but not me or Knox. Nevertheless, if we want our share of the income we have to do as he says.

"Fuck off," he roars before walking away.

"Why do you like pissing him off?"

"I don't. I like my money, that's it. Callan is fucking around and going to get us all in trouble if he doesn't pull his head out of Sandra's ass."

"Jealous, Steele? Oh, shit. You are huh?" Knox asks.

"Of Sandra? Fuck no. I could fuck her in the hall closet just like high school."

"You didn't?" His face is full of interest now. His blue eyes light up like a Christmas tree.

"The fuck I didn't. Right down the ninth hall, man." Slapping a hand on his shoulder, he laughs loudly as I turn and walk away when I see her. Tricia. She rushes toward me as she covers her lips in lip gloss. I want to roll my eyes but then I wouldn't be getting any pussy later. Instead, I let her push up against me, pressing her freshly glossed lips to mine.

"Where have you been?"

"Talking to Coach. Why?"

"Why are you always so short with me?" She flips her long blonde hair over her shoulder as she stares me down.

"You're too damn needy. That's why," I say as I try to walk past her. I don't get far which I already figured.

"You used to like it when I needed you."

"No, you thought I liked it," I remind her as she falls into step next to me. That's when I notice a girl I've never seen before standing outside with a cigarette between her lips. I tilt my head to the side and study her a second. There's no smoking allowed on campus but that doesn't mean that us guys couldn't do it. We can do anything.

"Who is she?" Tricia asks as she pulls her lipstick out of her purse.

"Don't know. I'm about to find out." Moving away from Tricia quickly, I walk out the side door and straight toward the girl. When I'm close enough, I grab the cigarette from her fingers, bringing it to my lips and inhaling. She looks up at me, light brown eyes bordering on the edge of anger.

"Didn't your mother teach you not to take things from others?" she asks cocking her head to the side to stare up at me.

"No. Actually, she taught me I should play nicely with others."

"And you think this is playing nicely?" I inhale another long drag before flicking it to the ground. Leaning down so I'm eye level with her, I blow the smoke in her face.

"One thing you will learn around here, new girl, is that we don't play nicely. Ever."

3

———

WHISPER

I make my way to the dance studio, yes, a dance studio in the damn academy. I was lucky to get into this class to begin with and the fact that I'm late isn't going to sit well with these uptight teachers. Not like I could have been on time in this giant ass maze of a school anyhow. As soon as I step in, everyone in the class stares.

"You must be Miss Sullens," the teacher says as she looks me up and down. I don't miss the look in her eye either. They aren't used to seeing people like me, apparently. Where most of the girls here wear fancy designer clothes, I'm walking around in torn jeans, combat boots and a band tee shirt.

"That's me," I say shoving my hands in my pockets.

"You're late. I don't appreciate you showing up to my class late," she snaps. I nod my head and walk to the corner of the room making sure to stand behind the other students. It isn't until the music starts playing that another guy walks in. He's tall, looks a lot like the one that took my cigarette earlier. Prick. He grins at the teacher and I watch as she just scowls back. That's when his eyes come to stop on me. His head tilts as he takes me in much the same as I'm doing to him. Then he moves. Right toward me as I uncap my water and take a long pull.

When he stops in front of me, I know we're going to have an issue. I can see the look in his eyes. He reaches up and takes my water from my hand bringing it to his lips, my mouth drops open. I reach up and snatch the bottle out of his hand causing some of to spill down his chin. He smiles and my heart nearly stops. Two dimples peek out of his cheeks.

"That wasn't very nice," he says, his tone sexual as hell. He drips sex appeal just like that other one but in a different way. Where this one is clearly a little friendlier, the other was dark and brooding.

"I'm not known for being nice. And to be honest, I don't know why you men around here think you can take whatever you want." Finding myself talking back to something as gorgeous as this man is a little strange.

"What does that mean?" he asks clearly intrigued by my words. I want to roll my eyes and walk away but there's something in his stare that makes me stay. Or maybe it's just the stupid side of me.

"It means first my cigarette and now my water. You men need to rethink who it is you're messing with," I add with a slight growl in my tone.

"Partners!" The teacher calls out as I drop my bottle onto my bag. As soon as I turn back, I'm in the arms of the man that pissed me off. He smirks and spins us around onto the dancefloor.

"I didn't say I wanted to partner with you," I hiss. He just chuckles and pulls my body closer to his. The music is fast; a hip-hop beat, yet he keeps me tucked closely to his hard frame.

"I don't ask, sweetheart. I just take, remember?" He grabs my wrist and spins me away from him before jerking me back in. His hips move, pressing into me as he dances. With a sigh and knowing that I'm not going to get out of this, I let him lead me. I let the music, the thump of the bass swirl through my body, taking control. My hips begin to move, my feet taking on a life of their own. In seconds, I'm lost in my own little world of dance and there is nothing or no one that could take this from me. The music keeps going and so do I. My partner grabs my hips, jerking me back into him. Our bodies move as one when suddenly the music stops.

Sweat drips down my temples as we both suck in air. Heaving for breath, our eyes clash when the teacher clears her throat. I step back, blinking rapidly.

"I wasn't aware you knew how to dance, Miss Sullens," she says as she walks closer to me and the mystery man.

"I… uh… I used to dance a lot back home. Not in a class or anything. More street dancing," I say. I hear a few laughs and giggles, but I don't give a shit. I'm not here for these stuck-up bitches.

"You move very freely. I think you'll do just fine in this class, although, we don't always have this type of music." I nod my head when her eyes move over my shoulder.

"Mr. Alder, we already knew you could dance. Showing off with the new girl isn't helping your grade at all." I turn my head to look at his face but all I see is that perfect grin.

"Mrs. Anderson, with all due respect, I'm your best dancer. The new chick has nothing on me." Asshole!

"We will see won't we, Knox." With that she walks away and leaves us standing in the middle of the room while she addresses the rest of the class.

"Don't get a big head. She only likes you because you're new," the man I know as Knox smarts off.

"There are few things about myself that I'm positive about and my dance skills are one of them. Watch your back, pretty boy," I tell him with a smirk. I turn to walk back to my bag, bending down to grab my water when large hands grip my waist. Before I can move, a hard cock is being thrust against my ass. The room erupts in laughter as the teacher tries to calm them. Knox leans over my back, brushing my hair over my shoulder with one hand and whispering in my ear, "They will all hate you soon. Then what will you do? You don't belong here, Miss Sullens and we will make sure you run as far from here as possible." As soon as he moves, I'm upright and ready for a fight but Knox is already halfway across the room heading for the door.

"Asshole," I grumble when the guy next to me laughs.

"You're not wrong. The Triple A's are all assholes." I bring my water to my lips and take another drink when I look over at him.

"What's the Triple A's?"

"The Alders. That was Knox, Callan is the youngest and then there's the oldest, Steele. They run this place. Or so they like to think. Stay out of their way and they won't bother you."

"And you are?" I ask raising an eyebrow.

"I'm Luke. Sorry," he adds holding his hand out to me.

"Whisper."

"That's your name?" a girl's voice sounds behind me. I glance over my shoulder and nod once. "Wow. And here I thought they didn't let trash in here."

"Excuse me?" I whirl around, squeezing the now empty water bottle in my hand.

"That could only be a name from a trailer park. We don't like trash, trailer girl." The words ring through my head but so does the thought of snapping her neck. I start to take a step toward her, ready to throw down if that's what I need to do when Luke grabs my wrist. He pulls me back and tosses his arm around my shoulder as he glares at her.

"Why don't you run along and find your kneepads, Tricia. I'm sure Steele is ready to be sucked off once again." I crack a smile. Maybe I'm going to like Luke.

"Oh, Luke. You should know better than to fuck with me. Steele will handle you," she says flipping her hair over her shoulder and walking away.

"Well, I would say that made a great first impression," Luke says as he pulls his arm away from me.

"I didn't mean to get you involved."

"Don't worry about it. Steele won't do shit. At least not to me. He knows Tricia is a web of lies."

"Don't like her much, huh?" I ask as I pick my bag up. I heard Mrs. Anderson dismiss the class early.

"She's one of those bitches you love to hate. She has a big crew here though, so once you piss her off her whole crew will hate you," he adds shrugging his bag over his shoulder.

"I'm not here to be liked. I don't really care if anyone likes me or not." We walk into the hallway when I spot Knox with the other asshole, then one more walks up. Jesus, they all look so similar.

"That's Steele and Callan. You met Knox," Luke adds.

"I met Steele too. Asshole stole my cigarette," I grumble.

"Yeah, there's no smoking on campus. Unless you're them," he chuckles.

"Good to know. I'll see you later, Luke."

"Where are you going?"

"To smoke a cigarette," I tell him with a smirk of my own. He chuckles and shakes his head before walking away. I stroll down the hall past the brothers from hell and out the side door, pulling a smoke free from the pack and lighting it up. Fuck the Triple A's. They don't scare me.

4

STEELE

I glance around the table at my brothers before bringing my eyes back to meet my dad's. I don't know why he's here and frankly I don't care.

"Why are your grades so low, Callan?" My eyes move to my brothers as I listen to the angry tone my dad uses.

"Practice has been running late. I'll get them up," my little brother adds.

"Yes, I know you will. My business doesn't deal with slackers as you very well know. If you ever want a chance to become the king of all this, you must have the right mindset."

"Lucky for us no one wants to be the king," I add.

"Steele! I will not tolerate that type of talk. I have groomed you boys to take over this company, this legacy, since you were born! I will not have you disrespecting it," he roars. Knox elbows me in the ribs as I sigh.

"Sorry. Can we just get on to what it is you want? You don't come home unless you need something from us." That part isn't a lie. We rarely see our dad and that doesn't bother me. I can't stand the man or the men he's trying to groom us into. I'd prefer to not have to deal with him at all if the choice were up to me.

"I've heard news that you're looking into the Macron family," he says setting his fork on the table next to his plate.

"And? You mentioned a job not long ago, and I wanted to make sure I had all the information I needed to handle it," I tell him casually.

"That isn't your decision to make, Steele. I tell you what you need to know. Now, if I hear one word of you snooping around again, I will make you pay for it." I ignore his threats. I've always ignored his threats because to be honest, I like his punishments. They give me a sick thrill of knowing what I can handle. He just doesn't know that part.

"What's the job?" Callan asks taking my dad's eyes off me.

"We've been informed that there is a new girl in the area. We aren't sure exactly how she fits in but she's here with the Weatherly's." Now that has my interests.

"They don't have kids and what the hell are they doing back in Rolling Springs?" I nearly growl.

"We don't know. They returned and have brought a child with them."

"And that has what to do with us?" Knox asks after being silent for most of the conversation.

"I'm about to tell you that. We have reason to believe that this girl isn't who they say she is," my dad says. Now that intrigues me. I sit up a little straighter, listen a little harder. My dad smirks knowing I like the sounds of that.

"And you want us to what? Make nice with her? Get her on our side and see what she knows?" I ask feeling the adrenaline as it rushes my system.

"Not exactly. If she is who we think she may be, we need information from her, not to scare her off." I shake my head. This doesn't make sense. Why would we want to get information from her? What information? As if he can read my mind, he continues, "We think she may have ties to the Macron family."

Callan lets out a long whistle, Knox sighs, and I stare right into my dad's eyes.

"Then why is it a problem for me to research them?"

"Because you don't need to! Why are you so damn stubborn, Steele?" I shrug.

"Like father, like son?" Knox chuckles.

"Don't keep this up. What I need for you to do is get close but not too close. We need to know anything she knows. You will be in charge of finding that out in any manner you see fit." Now that causes a spark of fire to ignite in my stomach. My lips slowly curl into a grin that both of my brothers understand. They both smile along with me as my dad shakes his head.

"Don't make me regret this," he adds.

"Oh, you won't regret it. If she knows anything, we will find out," I add. I grab my fork, stab it into a piece of steak and pop it into my mouth as multiple ideas form in my head.

"If you will excuse me, I have things to do. I'll be leaving again in the morning. I expect reports on this." I nod my head as my dad shoves out of his chair and walks off.

"Is it the new girl I saw in the hall? Dark hair?" Callan asks.

"That's her," I reply.

"Her name's Whisper. She's in dance. Not a bad dancer either. Her body is toned and tight." I jerk my head in Knox's direction wondering how exactly he knows that. He laughs. "We had to have partners, so I grabbed her." He shrugs making no apologies.

"I don't care what her body is like, we need to start planning out what we're going to do."

"Since when do we plan? We always just go with it," Callan

adds with a shrug of his own. I glance over my shoulder to make sure my dad isn't listening before leaning forward and resting my arms on the table.

"I'm not done looking into the Macron family. There's a reason this shit is all secretive and I want to know," I tell them. They both nod.

"So, we keep looking. We just do it on the down low. Dad won't find out anymore," Knox says. I nod as a smile crosses my face.

"Let's go pay our new girl a visit."

$$5$$

WHISPER

I've never had much luck with sleep. With sleep comes bad dreams. With bad dreams comes another sleepless night. I toss and turn trying to get comfortable in this plush bed. I don't think I've ever slept on anything so soft in my life. The Weatherly's made sure to go all out for me, but the way they sat at the dinner table tonight gave me chills. I didn't like how they looked at me, watched me. I think I was right. Psychos.

Throwing my legs over the edge of the bed, I stand and head for the door. I check to make sure their door is closed, which it is, before I walk down the steps. Making my way to the back door, I slip outside and inhale the cool night air. When I look up, I can see the stars. That's not something I'm used to either. Back home, I was in a big city, bounced from place to place. I was never in a place like this. As we were coming through town, Rolling Springs looked like a picturesque town that you would see on a TV show or in a magazine. Not a place I ever thought I'd be living. I take a deep breath and sit on the porch swing, closing my eyes as it sways. The swing dips and I can feel someone sitting next to me but I'm afraid to open my eyes.

"What do you want?" I ask softly, not knowing who it could be, but I assume it's Nathan or Debra.

"I'm not sure yet," a deep, dark voice says. I open my mouth to say more, my eyes snapping open, but before I can move or make a sound, a hand covers my mouth and an arm snakes around my body. I start to thrash, fight, but I'm lifted easily. I can make out two more shadows in the distance near the pool house as I'm manhandled and carried in that direction. I claw at the hands that hold onto me, kicking my feet but it does no good.

"Stop fighting," the man hisses into my ear. Yeah, that won't happen. It only makes me want to fight harder, and I try too.

In a few more long strides, we're in the pool house followed by the other two shadows. One of them slips something over my eyes before I'm being tossed onto a hard surface and my arms and legs tied down.

"You son of a bitch! I will kick your ass!" I scream before I'm being gagged. Well this isn't good.

"Calm down and I might take that off," one says in a hushed tone. I mouth around the gag when I feel hands on my body. They are tugging and ripping my clothes off. This isn't happening. Not again. Please, God, don't let this happen again! Tears burn the back of my eyes but I don't let them fall. I won't give them what they want. Instead, I remain perfectly still as my naked body is exposed to the cool air. Then there are hands on me. Roaming slowly over my flesh. Electric currents run from those hands and straight over my skin. What the hell is going on?

"I'm going to remove the gag and if you scream you aren't going to like what we do to you," one whispers in my ear. "Understand?" I nod my head rapidly when the gag is pulled free. Fingertips skate across the flesh of my stomach, bumps forming in their wake. I shouldn't be feeling this should I? They are basically going to rape me, and I feel like I'm high.

"Who are you?"

"Whisper," I say softly. Another hand comes to rest on my ankle, slowly rising up my leg to my thigh. I suck in a breath as another hand comes to my chest, slowly circling it.

"Who are your parents, Whisper?"

"I don't have any." That's the truth. My nipple is twisted and tugged as I moan. They think I'm lying? I don't have parents. Never have.

"Who do you live with?"

"Foster parents. They aren't my real parents." I gasp when another set of hands start slowly creeping over my stomach. If they were going to hurt me, why would they be asking these questions? Why aren't they just doing what they want?

"What's your last name?"

"Sullens," I say softly, feeling warm breath dance over my cheek. A warm tongue slips out, sliding up my cheek to my lips. Heat burns inside of me when lips cover mine. A kiss so hot I want to squeeze my thighs together. A dark chuckle sounds from down toward my legs as they're spread wider.

"Don't do this, please."

"Do what? Have a taste? We're not going to hurt you," the man says. I swallow hard when I feel hands move up my inner thighs and a man hum.

"You're wet," one whispers.

"Is she? I would think she likes this," another says right before I feel a tongue slip over my clit. I gasp and arch my back as much as I can, pressing into him. What is wrong with me? I've been in this position before, but I sure as hell didn't feel like this.

"All we want to know is who your real parents are, Whisper, and why you're here," the one near my head says.

"I don't know my real parents. I'm here for school." Soft lips wrap around my nipple, a wet tongue dancing and circling it. Hard sucks follow before a set of lips are back on mine. My body is buzzing. I don't think I've ever felt this high before. The three of them work me over until I'm trembling and on edge then it all just stops. I whimper and I hear a chuckle.

"You're lying. Who are you real parents?" I'm asked again. Don't I wish I knew? I never knew them. They dumped me off when I was just a baby. I was never adopted but no one ever knew why. I was tossed from place to place my whole life.

"I'm not. I don't know them."

"Why do you want to lie? We didn't want to hurt you, Whisper." My heart leaps into my throat when I hear the unmistakable sound of a switchblade being opened.

"I don't know anything!" The sharp tip of the blade rests on my inner thigh. Tears beg to be free but I blink them back. I won't let anyone else break me. I let it happen once but never again!

"You do know," the one by my legs says.

"You don't scare me," I say through gritted teeth. I hear them all chuckle around me as the tip slowly moves up between my legs. It barely touches my clit and I'm arching again. Fingers roughly spread me and the tongue is back. Flicking and lapping at me until I nearly combust.

"We aren't even done with you yet," the one by my head growls before devouring my lips once more. Another hand grabs my breast while lips suction over the other. Teeth bite down as I come in a swirl of lights blasting behind my eyes and tears rolling down my cheeks. The knife scrapes over my flesh causing a burning sting but it only intensifies what I'm already feeling. I hear the one by my head groan as he breaks the kiss and moves away from me. The hands and lips leave my chest but the one that just licked me is still breathing heavily against my thigh.

"This isn't how you were supposed to play but now that you've moved the pieces around the board, we will win." With that, my hands and legs are cut free. I'm still trembling from the orgasm when I try to shove myself up but it's too late. The door slams to the pool house and they are gone. I slowly push up once more in a daze trying to figure out what just happened here. My body is still tingling as I climb up and stand. Grabbing a towel that's hanging nearby, I wrap it around my body and move toward the door. Peeking out, I want to make sure they're gone before I step foot outside. When I'm satisfied that they are, I run toward the house and in the back door. I'm up the stairs and locked in the safety of my room before I let the waterworks start. Each hot tear that slips down my cheek hurts. I know what my life was like before and I never want to go back to that. This was supposed to be my chance at a new life. A new town.

Walking into the bathroom, I flip the light on and then the shower. As I stare at myself in the mirror, I wonder who they were. Why would they think I was lying about who I am? Don't they think that I'd love to know who my parents were? That I would love to have some kind of family that was actually mine? I close my eyes and fight the urge to cry once more. I've shed enough tears throughout my life that I don't have many left to spare. Instead of letting them fall, I climb in the shower and wash away what happened tonight. What I let happen. How could I have been so stupid? What was I thinking? The burn on my thigh causes me to look down. There, right where the blade was is a small cut that has since stopped bleeding.

"How did he know that I would like that?" I whisper to myself.

6

STEELE

"This is all bullshit," I hiss as I fling another file at my brothers. Knox grabs it up and flips through the contents as Callan sits back with a joint between his lips.

"You know what's bullshit? Being up this early. We don't have school for another hour, Steele," he whines.

"Do I look like I give a shit? Take a fucking nap, slacker." He rolls his eyes and inhales before passing the joint to Knox.

"There is no way that this is everything there is on the Macron family. There has to be more somewhere," Knox chimes in.

"I'm sure there is but where?" I snap, running my hand through my hair. We've been here for hours in one of my dad's offices. Not his home office because I already know that there's nothing in there. He isn't that stupid to leave things around where we can get our hands on them.

"I don't know. Years ago, no one used computers to keep tabs, right? So there has to be a paper trail somewhere," Callan adds. I sit back in the leather chair and glance around the small office. It isn't here. Whatever it is I'm looking for is not here. I can feel it.

"We still handling that other shit tonight?" Knox asks.

"Yeah. Dad wants that shit destroyed so we destroy it."

"Anyone else getting really tired of what dad wants?" I'm shocked when Callan is the one that says that. Both Knox and I look at him strangely. "What?" he asks bringing his water to his lips.

"Since when do you not want what Dad has?"

"I didn't say I didn't want it. I said I'm sick of doing what he says. There's a big difference, Steele. He's always on our asses to do this or that for the business but we never know shit. I can't be the only one that pisses off," he tells us.

"Why do you think we're here?" I ask, raising an eyebrow. I get what he's saying and I agree. It's only a matter of time before we uncover all the secrets and then we set our plan into motion. At the end of the day, our game plan is the same as it has been for years. They, being the founding members, just don't know it yet. Shoving to my feet, I slip the files back where they belong and motion for my brothers to follow me. We step out the door and are greeted with the last person I wanted to see.

"Ah, the Alder boys," he says with a smile on his face. Old bastard.

"Mr. McLean. How are you today?" I ask before biting the inside of my cheek to keep myself from saying what I really feel.

"All is well. What are you boys doing here?" He looks between the three of us and I have to stop myself from rolling my eyes or snapping his neck.

"We were just stopping by to see Dad when I remembered he was leaving this morning. I thought maybe he would have stopped by here before he left," I lie. It's so easy to lie. They have instilled that in us since we were small kids.

"I see. Is there anything you needed? Maybe I can assist?" Shaking my head, Callan chuckles behind me. The dumb, high fuck.

"No. We were just going to say goodbye. We really need to be getting to school."

"That's right. All the Alder boys are college men now. How's that going? How is football? I plan on making the next game as well as the mayor," he adds. The fucking mayor. Yeah, if you count his stupid son as the Mayor of Rolling Springs then sure. I personally hate the little fuck. He may be Mayor but that doesn't mean shit to us. We still control him.

"How is your son, Blake?" He hates it when I call his son by his name and not Mayor. Hence the reason I do it. I see the way his eyes narrow slightly.

"He's well. Just won the recent elections." I nod and start to walk past him when Callan adds, "Suppose there wasn't much competition." The three of us laugh as we walk down the stairs and out the front door of the building.

"I can't stand that fucker," Knox hisses.

"No shit. I hate Blake. One day I'll take that fucker down." The guys all laugh as we climb into my SUV. I shove the key in the ignition and shift into drive. Watching my rearview mirrors, I see him in the door.

"We're being watched," I say as I keep my eyes on him.

"Seriously?" Knox snaps.

"Yeah. Fuck, this is going to get out of hand," Callan adds.

"No, it's not. We tell Dad that we were picking up the files on Rasper." That will keep us off his shit list, anyway.

The drive to school doesn't take long and I groan out loud when we get there. I don't want to be in school. I don't want to go to college but these are the necessary evils in our lives. At least for the moment.

We all climb out as I heft my bag onto my shoulder and turn to look at my brothers. Without the two of them, I don't know where I'd be. We are each other's keepers. We have each other's backs even when we're pissed. Nothing can pull us apart.

"I'll talk to you guys later. Going to see Ray," I inform them. They both nod, their eyes already drifting to some of the girls that are walking past. I shake my head and walk inside and straight through the hall when I see her. Pulling my switchblade out, I step up behind her and flick it open. The sound couldn't be mistaken, and neither was her little jolt.

"What's up, Luke? Find a new girl?" I ask when I see him right in front of her.

"Yeah, she's new." She slowly turns and looks up at me with wide eyes that quickly narrow. Anger shines in those light brown irises.

"New toys are always fun," I say keeping my eyes on hers. She opens her mouth like she's about to say something when I lean down close to her ear. "Switchblades are the sneakiest little knives ever, aren't they?" She sucks in a breath before I pull back and walk away, shoving my blade back in my pocket.

"Was it you?" she yells down the hallway. I ignore her and keep walking when I hear feet hitting the floor behind me. I know it's her following me so when I round the corner, I'm ready for her. She comes around right behind me and I grab and pull her into the first empty classroom behind me. She doesn't have a chance to move, or scream. One hand pushes her against the door, the other over her mouth.

"You shouldn't fuck with strangers, Whisper. It's danger-ous," I whisper, my lips so close to her flesh. I remember the taste of her sweet pussy from the other night. The way she melted on my tongue. Fuck, I will never get that taste of out my head.

"Was it you?" she asks when I pull my hand free.

"Was what me?" I ask tilting my head to the side and studying her face.

"In the pool house, asshole. Was it you?" she asks again gritting her teeth.

"What were you doing in the pool house, Whisper? Does Mommy and Daddy know?" Her eyes catch fire as she bucks against me trying to push me away. Not a chance in hell.

"They aren't my parents," she hisses.

"I know they aren't your real parents, but I want to know who is."

"Is that why you came after me last night?"

"Aren't you just full of questions today? Let me ask you this. If I were to say it was me, then what? What would you do?" Those eyes. Damn, I like the fire in them.

"You bastard. I will find out and when I do, I will make you pay for it." Her anger is warranted although it means nothing to me. I don't care what she has to say. She is our target, we're not hers.

"I don't know, Whisper. I think you enjoyed it," I whisper closely to her face. Slowly, I lower my mouth to hers, letting it linger there. Her eyes never leave mine as we both breathe heavily against each other. I move first, slowly pressing my lips to hers. Kissing her is something else. She fights my lips at first before eventually giving in to me. Our tongues collide and heat races through me. My cock swells in my jeans when I jerk away from her. She's panting and her eyes are wild. I can smell her wetness from here. She's attracted to me, that much I'm sure of.

"You have a thing for danger?" I ask her, letting my lips curl into a smirk.

"You have a thing for unwilling girls?" she challenges with her eyebrow raised. Stepping back into her, I reach around and grab the door handle.

"I didn't hear anyone protesting." With that, her eyes widen, and I open the door sending her falling to her ass in the hall in front of everyone.

"Next time you may want to try kissing someone that wants it," I announce to half the people walking past. Most just laugh and go on about their business but it's Tricia that I saw first. Her big blue eyes widen as she storms toward Whisper. She's climbing off the floor as I lean against the wall with my arms crossed over my chest watching the show.

"You tried to kiss him?" Tricia's squeal sounds through the hall as she pulls her hand back and slaps Whisper across the face. It doesn't take long for that fight to ensue. Whisper smirks and then lunges for Tricia. Just as I see Whisper's face contort in anger, Knox and Callan are there pulling them apart. Whisper never got the chance to swing.

"What the hell?" Knox roars shoving Tricia in my direction. "You were just going to watch that shit?" he asks, directing his anger toward me. I shrug my shoulders as Tricia presses her body into mine.

"It was interesting," I add.

"Really? We have a job to do, Steele!" Knox roars as I glance over at Callan. He has Whisper pinned against the wall, whispering words in her ear. Her eyes stay on mine the whole time but as she nods her head, something inside of me grinds and shreds. I want to snap her neck, but even more? I want to taste her on my tongue again.

7

———

WHISPER

This day was interesting. Surprisingly, no one called me to the office over the little altercation in the hallway. If Callan hadn't pulled me back, I would have torn her face off. Now I'm in the dance room doing my own thing. Words float from my lips as I sing at the top of my lungs. I made sure to check that no one was around first. The music thumps through the speakers and I let myself go. If anything can calm me, it's singing and dancing. Those are the two things that I've always used to keep my head straight. I started dancing when I was just three. I remember hearing hip-hop music outside and when I went to look, there were a ton of people dancing around a radio. One of the older girls smiled and motioned for me to join them. I did and I've been dancing ever since.

"You sure can move your ass." I jerk, ready to move when hands wrap around my waist. Looking over my shoulder, I see it's Callan and let out a breath.

"Are you stalking me?" I ask raising an eyebrow.

"Nah. I was walking past and looked in and saw you.

Where'd you learn to dance and sing like that?" He releases my hips as I turn to face him.

"On the streets." I shrug.

"You learned to sing on the streets? I highly doubt that," he muses.

"I did. I was never in one place long enough to go to classes," I tell him. Why am I admitting this to him? He's one of them. He has to be one of the ones that were in the pool house with me. Yet, there is something so calm and caring in his eyes that I feel like I could trust him with anything.

"Foster kid?" he asks cocking his head and waiting.

"Yeah. All my life."

"What? You were never adopted?" he asks in disbelief. I shake my head but keep quiet. "That... wow. I'm sorry."

"Don't be. I'm not."

"You never wondered?"

"Why I wasn't adopted?" I ask. Callan nods. "Yeah. Wouldn't you? There is nothing, well there was nothing wrong with me back then. I would watch all the other kids being adopted but no one ever came to see me."

"Ever?"

"Nope. I just learned to move from place to place and not ask questions," I tell him.

"That had to be hard. Knowing no one wanted you." The way he says it... it's different. It's not an I'm sorry type of response and it's not quite a jab at me either. Either way, I take a step back when he counters it. His hands find my hips once more and his fingers dig into my flesh. I gasp as his eyes meet mine. The music on my phone changes and Callan begins to move with me. I knew Knox could dance since he's in my class, but Callan moves just as perfectly as his brother. The beat starts to hit and we both break apart. Callan follows my lead, popping and swaying. I watch him in the mirrors in front of us, entranced by his movements. He reaches over his shoulder and pulls his shirt off in one move, tossing it to the side as he keeps going. I gasp, watching the tan muscles as they work. Callan is well built, looking like a damn god and I assume his brothers aren't far behind. Our eyes stay locked as we both dance freely when I hear the door slam. I jolt and spin around coming face to face with Steele and Knox.

"What is this? A little private lesson?" Steele asks moving toward us. Callan laughs, reaches down and grabs his shirt, tossing it over his shoulder as he moves.

"Just having some fun before practice," Callan says, pushing through the door and disappearing while the other two come closer. I turn, ready to grab my stuff when I'm pushed against the mirror. My eyes lock with Steele's and the air escapes my lungs. Knox moves in next to him, just as imposing as his brother.

"Having a little fun?" Steele asks, pressing his cock into my ass. My breathing is still coming in heaves from my dance.

"Not with you I'm not." Steele chuckles darkly as Knox smirks.

"We're a fun group, me and my brothers. We like playing together with our toys, if you know what I mean." That came from Knox. I nearly roll my eyes because I'm almost one hundred percent sure that they were the ones in the pool house that night, but I can't say that for sure.

"Well, I guess that's too bad, I'm not interested." Knox's eyes light up but he doesn't say anymore. When I drag my gaze back to Steele's there's something darker in them. A challenge of sorts.

"What were you doing with my brother?" he asks pressing into me harder.

"We were dancing."

"So I see. You think you can just walk in here and get in my brother's good graces?" I shake my head before it's slammed into the glass mirror. I wince but I don't let him see how much it hurt me.

"Fuck you," I taunt, knowing that it's going to piss him off a little more. His hand slips around my stomach, easing into the front of my yoga pants as he hums.

"You want me to fuck you, Whisper?" Knox chuckles again but I can't take my eyes off Steele. He's messing with my head, getting inside and I can't let that happen.

"Not if you were the last dick on earth."

"Is that why you're so wet?" he huffs in my ear. His eyes dance in the mirror, a silent song that I'd love to sing but know that I can't hit the keys.

"I'll scream," I warn him.

"Go ahead. We like screamers," Knox sneers as I open my mouth. Just before anything comes out, Steele's hand is gone and he's turned heading for the door. I spin around and watch both of them as they leave the way they came when another girl walks in.

"Hey." I don't smile or acknowledge her because frankly, I've had my fair share of Alder Academy assholes for the day. Spinning around, I grab my bag and start to walk away when she speaks again, "I saw what they did."

"And?" Now I do turn to face her.

"They're like that with everyone. They think they own the world," she says rolling her eyes.

"Don't they?" I ask raising my eyebrow.

"Not if you don't let them. You have to fight back."

"And you know this from experience?" She giggles and shakes her head.

"Hell no! My family is a transplant to the area. I made it

through the asshole stage a few years ago. I was in senior year of high school with Callan." Now that has piqued my interests. Maybe she will be a valuable ally to me.

"So, where do I start? How do I get them to back off?" I ask curiously. I want to know what she has to say and any insight into the three assholes.

"First, you show up everywhere they are. That really bugs them," she says with a smile.

"How exactly does that work?" She laughs and walks toward me, resting her hand on my shoulder. I look from her hand to her face wondering what the hell she's doing.

"They see you. That drives them insane. The whole point of fucking with you is to make you invisible. What a better way to not let them do that." She has a point. A very good one at that.

"What's your name?" I ask curious now.

"Shane. I know, boy's name, girl body."

"I actually like it, Shane. I'm Whisper."

"I know who you are. We all know who you are. New girl on campus. Word flies around here like flies on shit."

"So, when do we start?"

"Start?" she asks, cocking her head to the side.

"Yeah, being seen." A smile crosses my face for the first time since I've been here. I like the sound of pushing back.

"Oh, we can do that right now. Football practice." Linking her arm with mine, she leads me out of the dance room and into the hall.

"Football, huh?"

"Yep. All three of them. I don't really like them due to their smug-ass attitudes, but I will say they are some damn good play-ers. Even Callan and he's a freshman," Shane tells me. I'm not so shocked that they play football. They are well built and solid. At least what I've felt of them.

I follow Shane outside and around the walkway before we're headed down toward the field. She pulls a badge free and flashes it at the man standing near the gates. He nods and allows us through.

"What was that?"

"Practices are closed unless you're certain people. The paper being one." She smirks and wiggles her eyebrows.

"And you just happen to be on the paper, right?" I laugh a little.

"Yeah, you can say a certain Alder and I were kinda together for half a minute years ago." Holy shit!

"Which one?" Her cheeks blush as she guides me to the stands and sits. I follow next to her but I don't let her off that easily. This I need to know.

"Callan. He blew me off once college started. Acts like he doesn't even know who the hell I am anymore," she adds a little sadly. Shane is pretty. Not who you'd picture on the school paper or anything because to me that's always the dorky kids that have no social lives, but maybe I'm wrong. Shane has long blonde hair that has light curls hanging down her back and big blue eyes that gleam when she smiles. Now that I think about it, she doesn't look like anyone that would be caught dead hanging out with me either. It makes me a little nervous until I follow her stare. That's when I see it. The three Alder boys staring dead at us.

"Holy shit," I whisper under my breath. Shane laughs.

"Exactly. See how much fun this could be?" She nudges me with her elbow making me smile along with her. The coach yells something and the three of them turn back to what they were doing.

Yeah, I think Shane and I are going to get along just fine.

8

———

STEELE

"Where the hell is he?" Callan whines for the fourth time in ten minutes. The boy has no self-control when it comes to these jobs. He's impatient and it annoys me.

"Would you shut up? Just sit back and enjoy the night air," I hiss in his direction. I adjust my leather gloves when I hear talking. Raising my hand, I silence the two of my brothers. Knox moves closer as we watch the men in front of us talking and shaking hands.

"He's got company," Knox whispers.

"How many?" Callan asks shifting closer.

"Just the one. We got him," Knox adds. I nod my head and motion for them to move. Coming out of the bushes I stand tall as we walk toward them. Rasper turns around and spots us, his eyes widening.

"Steele, what are you doing here?" he asks as if he doesn't already know.

"Oh, come on, Rasper. You want to play that game?" I ask

cocking my head to the side. I never did like this fucker. His eyes move from me to my brothers before quickly glancing to his little friend. With one quick nod of my head, Callan moves to grab the man.

"He has nothing to do with this!" Rasper roars. I smirk and shake my head.

"You're in Rolling Springs. That makes him our business, doesn't it?" Knox asks stepping up next to me. The guy Callan has doesn't fight him which is funny. If I saw the three of us at night, I for damn sure would fight.

"Let him go, Steele. Whatever you want, I'll do it. Just let him go."

"It doesn't work that way, Rasper." I pull my fist back, slamming it into his stomach. He doubles over gasping for air as Callan releases the man that he's had a hold on. Fists fly, mainly from us until they both lie on the ground bleeding.

"He dead?" I ask Knox. He leans down, pressing his fingers to Rasper's neck before shaking his head. With a sigh, I reach down, grab the front of his shirt and raise his head, throwing another punch. This time I hear bones crushing. Once I'm satisfied that they are both handled, we turn to leave when I see it.

"Someone's watching," I say keeping my voice low. All of us know better than to turn and look.

"Where?" Callan asks.

"Our three o'clock." I laugh out loud and start walking back toward the SUV when Knox curses under his breath.

"What?"

"It's her."

"Her who?" I nearly growl.

"Whisper." He says her name softly. The thought of her seeing what we did makes my cock hard. I shift like I'm going to turn and talk to my brothers, but my eyes lock with hers instead.

The silent showdown between us is hot. I can feel each little buzz of energy that wafts off the two of us.

"We can't kill her," Callan says.

"No. We need her," I say keeping my eyes glued to hers. Strangely I don't see the fear in her that I would see in most people that witnessed something like that. All I see is intrigue and curiosity. Her head slowly tilts to the side as if she's trying to figure me out. She won't. When I raise my hand and bring it to my throat, drawing a line, she gets it. Her mouth snaps closed, and she turns quickly disappearing into the night as I watch.

"That was… nice." Knox chuckles.

"It was something. Let's get out of here before the sheriff shows up. I don't feel like dealing with him tonight." I pull my gloves off as we climb in the car.

"You don't think she'd say anything do you?" Callan asks.

"I don't know, Cal. She isn't one of us." The thought crossed my mind a few times but each time I blew it off. She isn't stupid by any means. She has to know now what she's up against and I don't think she's going to be that dumb as to try and cross us anymore.

"She won't say anything. She isn't stupid," Knox states what I was already thinking. I pull my phone out and dial our dad, listening to it ring.

"Is it done?" No, hi or anything, straight to business.

"It's done. Had someone with him. Took care of him too."

"Who was it?"

"I didn't stick around to ask names," I growl into the line.

"That's great, Steele! Go around killing unknown people! That's exactly what we need!" I close my eyes and take a deep breath trying to control the anger that simmers inside of me.

"What should we have done? Let him walk?" My jaw clenches, my teeth grinding painfully together. Before he even answers me, the line goes dead. I already know what that means. I lower the phone and close my eyes.

"He hung up?" Knox asks.

"Yeah."

"Fuck," Callan curses.

"You two stay out of this," I warn them both. They are both about to say something when I jerk my gaze around to them. "I mean it. You stay out it! I'll take it!"

"We have a game coming up, Steele," Knox reminds me. No shit. How could I ever forget that?

"And?"

"And you need to be in perfect condition. You aren't taking this shit alone," Callan responds. I reach over and grab him around the throat, pulling his face closer to mine.

"I said, I'm taking it. All of it! Don't push me on this," I growl. Callan watches me intently for a long second before he finally nods his head. I release the hold I have on him and take a deep breath before starting the car. I reach for the radio and turn it up, listening to Slipknot as I let the rest of the world fade away.

Before we even pull into the driveway, I see the dark SUVs.

"He was fast about it this time," Knox says from the backseat. I nod my head, listening to the music as I stare out the front window at my fate. Inhaling through my nose, I shut the car off and climb out. Knox and Callan aren't far behind me.

We walk as one toward the house when they all step out the front door. Their eyes are as black as night, which is something I'm used to. These are the men that your parents warn you about. The monsters that lurk in the dark. We might be bad, but these guys are far worse. They are my dad's top men and when they show up, you know shit's bad. The main one, Matt, eyes me up and down. He knows I'm a fighter. He knows what I'm capable of, so when it's only me taking the punishment, he enjoys it far more. Not that my brothers can't fight, they can but they have smaller builds than me.

"Well look what we have here," Matt says with a sick grin on his face. "The three bastards."

"It's only me," I announce, catching his attention. He turns his head, his eyes meeting mine. A slow sick smirk crosses his face.

"That sounds fun." I nod my head once, getting myself into the headspace I need to be in for this.

"Callan, Knox. Go inside," I say keeping my eyes on Matt. He smirks as the two of them walk past us and into the house.

"Meet you in the basement," Matt says turning on his heel. His guys all follow him as I take another deep breath and prepare myself for what's about to come.

9

WHISPER

"How are you liking Alder?" Debra asks all happily. It makes me want to vomit. This fake front she puts up for the world to see—I can see right through it.

"It's school," I say, picking at my eggs. I don't know why she decided today would be the day for a family breakfast but here we are.

"Are you making friends?" Nathan asks.

"With those stuck-up rich kids? I don't think so."

"Excuse me?" Debra squeals. "We brought you here, took you in and that's how you thank us? By talking that way?"

"What can I say, Debra? You shouldn't have done it. I didn't ask to be here. You should have left me there to rot." In seconds, she's out of her chair, her hand slamming across my cheek. Crazy bitch. I shove out of my seat, ready to challenge her but think better of it. Our eyes lock and a silent warning is issued.

"That's enough! Now, Whisper, you apologize, or I can arrange for a nice comfortable bed in our local jail!" Nathan's voice thunders through the room. I swallow my pride, if only for a second and say sorry. Not that I really mean it because if she ever lays her hand on my again, I'm going to lose it. Debra smiles like she's won the big prize at the fair which makes me want to slap her more.

"Can I go? I don't want to be late." Nathan nods his head as I move from the table and grab my bag.

"You don't need to push her. We will get what she knows soon, Debra!" I hear Nathan say. What is he talking about? I don't know anything aside from this place is hell. Ignoring their talk, I head out the door and down the long driveway. I walk to school every day. Nathan offered me a car to drive but Debra said I didn't earn it. Imagine that, after a month of being here and doing as I'm told, and I didn't earn the right to drive to school.

Ignoring the pesky feelings in the back of my head, I walk down the sidewalk a little lost in my own world. Maybe I would be better off in jail. Maybe that's where I belong. This city is warped and not in a good way. The Alder brothers are warped. Everything around here is shady. It's almost like living in the twilight zone.

"Ahh, you shouldn't be walking all alone." I close my eyes, take a deep breath and ignore Callan's voice. I hear the vehicle pulling up but like most of the time, I ignore that too.

"He's right. It's not safe," Knox responds. I can tell them apart by just their voices now. That was an easy one. After all the tormenting they've done to me over the last month, how could I not? From sicking their little girl tribes on me while I'm in the bathroom to outright harassing me in the hallways. Just last week, Steele made it look like we were about to have sex in the cafeteria in front of everyone only to shove me off him causing me to slam into someone else. They think they can break me, but they can't. I won't let them.

"We live in the Mayberry equivalent, I think I'm fine," I call out over my shoulder not bothering to look back. That's when I feel him. Steele is behind me; I know he is but I don't look back. I just keep walking. I never brought up what I saw that night, not that I needed to. They remind me daily that if I say anything, I will end up like those men. I just brush them off and keep doing what I do every day of my life.

When a hand clamps down on my hip, I wince and stop walking.

"Why'd you stop?" Steele whispers in my ear. The hairs on the back of my neck stand on end but that shiver that races through me? Yeah, he noticed that much.

"What do you want, Steele?"

"That's a loaded question, Whisper." His lips move slowly over my neck and I nearly gasp. This asshole knows what he's doing to me.

"You winced when he grabbed you. Why?" Knox is in my face now. I close my eyes and let out a breath before opening them and locking with his big blue ones.

"Umm, it hurt?"

"Since when?" Steele asks over my shoulder.

"I don't know, since your hands are huge, and you gripped me like I was falling from the sky?" I snap. In seconds, he has me spun around, his hands coming to the top of my jeans. I start to move but one nod of his head and Knox has me pinned against him.

"What the hell?" Callan asks as he climbs out of the car coming toward us. Steele pulls my jeans down one side over my hip before he gasps.

"What happened?" Callan asks looking up at me with sincerity in his eyes. Yeah, what a lie that is.

"I fell."

"No, you didn't. You're one of the most coordinated people I've ever seen," Knox growls behind me.

"I was trying new moves. It happens." I shrug against his hold.

"Don't lie to us, Whisper." The growl that rumbles through Steele's chest has my pussy clenching. I hate that he affects me the way he does. I hate that all of them affect me in some sort of way.

"Maybe it happened when you pushed me into the table last week," I say raising an eyebrow at Steele. His face, usually a mask of darkness and anger quickly morphs into something else. Something I've never seen before. Is that regret? For pushing me? No, not coming from these three it isn't.

"Is that true? Did it happen when he pushed you?" Callan asks getting right in my face.

"No, asshole! It didn't, so calm down and let me go. I'm going to be late." Knox releases his hold on me, and I shrug my bag back up my shoulder. I start to move past them when I'm grabbed from behind and lifted off my feet.

"Put me down! What is wrong with you?" I roar as Steele carries me to the car. Tossing me in like I'm a rag doll, he climbs in behind me. The other two get in up front as Steele stares into my eyes. Then he moves. His hands are all over me, tugging at my clothes, half ripping them off my body. I try to fight him back, fight him off me but it does no good.

"Stop! What are you doing?" I scream as he continues. I look to Knox for help but he's watching it all take place.

"Where else?" Steele growls.

"Where else what?" I ask as he pulls my shirt up.

"The bruises, Whisper! Where else do you have bruises!" he roars in my face. I try to shove my shirt down the best I can when his fingers press into the bruise near my rib.

"Ouch!" I hiss as I try to scoot away. This time he lets me.

"She has more," Steele says looking to Knox.

"Who did that to you?" Knox asks looking back at me.

"I fell. I told you that." Steele reaches over once more, slower this time. His fingers move softly over my skin until they linger on the bruise. He looks up into my eyes and my heart leaps into my throat. That stare. The pools of ocean blue that swirl in them, it's consuming. I open my mouth about to say more but quickly close it again. He doesn't like that. His fingers press into the bruise causing me to whimper.

"I'll find out, Whisper. I find out everything," he says leaning in closer to me.

"There's nothing to find out. I told you what happened."

"Lies. You told me a bunch of lies."

"Were they?" I ask tilting my head to the side to look at him. Why does he have to be so powerful? Why does his scent, his cologne make me dizzy? What is it with these three that call to me like a drug that I want to get my hands on? Luckily, I don't have to think too long. The car comes to a stop and I'm out the door before Steele has the chance to move. Rushing inside, I glance over my shoulder and take a breath.

"That was interesting," Shane says as she steps up next to me.

"It was weird."

"You rode to school with them?" she asks, raising an eyebrow.

"Not exactly. More like I was kidnapped." Rolling my eyes, she laughs as we walk down the hallway. I'm still a little unsure of what was happening in the car as we step into our English class. Luke greets us quickly, coming up to me.

"Hey. You have a good weekend?"

"Yeah. It was… fine. You?" He nods his head and smiles as

we make our way to our seats. We all sit, and I pull out my notebook and pen when the door slams loudly. We all jump and look just in time to see Steele strolling through the room.

"What's he doing in here? This isn't his class," Luke mumbles under his breath. That's when Steele turns his head and looks directly at me. A shiver runs through my body as I look away first. Whatever it is he's doing, I want no part of it. I can feel his intensity when he sits behind me. I keep looking forward. I refuse to turn around and look at him. I won't do it. I won't give him the satisfaction of knowing that he's affecting me.

The TA starts talking, telling us that the professor is out for the day and that he's taking over the class. I try to focus, pay attention to the notes he's giving us when I feel Steele's hand on my shoulder. I nearly jump out of my skin at the contact.

"Why so jumpy?" he whispers in my ear. I cut my eyes to the left to see if Luke is paying attention, but he isn't or at least he's acting like he isn't.

"Why are you in here?"

"Who put those bruises on you?"

"We've already discussed this," I remind him.

"Was it Luke? Did your new little boyfriend hurt you?" I spin around in my seat listening to Shane giggle under her breath as I come face to face with Steele. He's leaning in so closely that our lips nearly touch. The mint on his breath assaults my nose as I look into his eyes.

"I don't have a boyfriend, nor do I want one. I told you, I fell."

"Don't make this harder on yourself or him, Whisper. I will find out," he nearly growls. He leans in, his lips touching mine. God, why do they have to feel so good? Why does his touch send fire through my veins? Then his words hit me. Don't make this harder on him? He won't touch Luke. I won't let him. With that anger now eating away at me, I bite down into Steele's lip. He lets out a growl that has the whole class turning to see what's happening. He pulls back, reaches up and wipes the blood on his hand as he smiles. No, that isn't a smile. That's a dark promise of what's going to happen. I just stirred the sleeping bear in him.

"You okay?" Luke leans in as I stay still, watching Steele.

"I'm fine."

"But are you really?" Steele asks loud enough that half the room hears him. "Or do you like it when I reject you in front of everyone?" Girls giggle and the guys howl. My eyes narrow as I try to figure out what his game is.

"Mr. Alder! I'm in the middle of a class," the TA says loudly.

"Oh, do forgive me, Mr. Tyler. I wasn't aware that you were teaching today. Please, do go forth and teach us." He mocks the man. The class laughs once more. "Or would you prefer to demonstrate instead?"

"What are you talking about, Steele?" Mr. Tyler asks. I can see the sweat trickle down his temples from here. He shouldn't push Steele like that. What the hell is he thinking?

"You know, the fun you have on the weekends," Steele implies as he walks down the steps toward the front of the room. "I've heard that whips and sex swings are involved," he adds. Mr. Tyler turns white as a ghost.

"Stop this!"

"Stop what? They may be interested in the sordid games you play," Steele says. I can see Mr. Tyler swallow hard as Steele moves behind him. Grabbing the back of his neck, he pushes him down onto the desk at the front of the room. My heart is hammering in my chest. I can't believe that he's doing this to him. What is wrong with him?

"Something like this?" Steele growls as he rocks his hips, air fucking the teacher on the desk. I can see tears filling the TA's eyes as the class roars in laughter. How could he do this to him? What did he do to deserve this? Abandoning my things, I leap from my seat and run down the stairs and out the door when strong arms catch me. Tears cloud my vision as memories slam into me.

"Whisper? What's wrong?" Oh God. That was me. That was me on that desk only it wasn't. Why is this happening now? I thought I was over all of that. I thought I moved past it! Anger at myself is almost consuming me. I'm being lifted in someone's arms and carried but my head is a mess. I don't know what's happening to me.

"Whisper, look at me," Callan pleads. Sobs clog my throat right before lips come down on mine. This kiss is soft, gentle even. I blink rapidly trying to stop the tears when I see him. Pulling back, I shove at his chest causing him to stumble back.

"Don't touch me!" I scream looking around for an exit when the door flies open again. Steele and Knox both step in, closing the door behind them. It's one of the study rooms. I've been here before. There's only one way out and they're blocking it. My chest heaves. There isn't enough oxygen in the room for all of us. My mouth opens and closes but nothing is happening.

"What the hell happened?" Callan asks looking to his brothers.

"A little presentation in English class." Steele smirks. My mouth is dry. I can't swallow. I feel like my throat is closing up as I grip the edge of the table behind me.

"She freaked out. What did you do?" Callan asks turning to Steele. The both of them talk but I can't hear them. What the hell? What's happening to me?

"Please," I whisper but it comes out hoarse. They can't hear me. I can't hear me. My head swims as memories rush me and then I'm falling.

"Shit!" I hear Knox yell. I hit the floor, my head bouncing off the tiles as the room spins.

"What happened?"

"I don't know!" Knox roars. Hands touch my face, my chest. Another hand runs through my hair. Everything is cloudy, I can't see their faces.

"Whisper? What's happening?" I hear Callan ask. I open my mouth, but nothing comes out. Am I dying? Is this what dying feels like?

"Whisper? Whisper!"

10

STEELE

"Someone has been beating her," the doctor says eyeing me like I did it. I growl and grind my teeth before Knox steps in front of me.

"We pay you, Doc. Remember that shit the next time you're about to accuse one of us of something." The old grey-haired man nods his head and steps back.

"She needs to rest. She had a pretty severe panic attack from what you're telling me. She will probably sleep it off for quite some time. Give her these when she wakes up to help the headache, I'm sure she will experience," he says passing Knox a bottle of pills.

"What caused it?" Callan asks, clearly concerned. Over the last month, things have shifted with her. I didn't want to say much but I can feel it. I don't want to hurt her, push her anymore. I want her on her back under me. I want to feel her lips on mine. Every time I see her with anyone else, I feel this need to claim her even though I know that's not what I need to be doing. It doesn't matter though.

"It's really hard to say until she's awake and we can ask her. Maybe she saw something that triggered a memory or smelled something. There are many reasons this could have happened." I eye Knox as he watches me. This is my fault. Whatever I did in that classroom triggered her but why? What happened to her?

"And the bruises?" Knox asks pulling his eyes from mine.

"They are new. I see some signs of older ones as well but mainly new. It appears that she once had a broken rib at some point in her life."

"What?" I roar spinning to face him.

"Her injury was either treated poorly or not treated at all. There's a little unevenness there on the right side." My throat feels tight as I drag my gaze back to her lying on my bed. I vaguely hear the doctor say something else to Knox before he leaves. That's when a hand comes down on my shoulder.

"What are you thinking?" Callan asks.

"What the hell are we doing to her?"

"What we were told to do," Knox replies.

"But why? She clearly has no idea what we want from her or at least she isn't letting on. Maybe we need a new approach," I say, stunning myself with the words. I've never been one to back down from a fight. I've never been one to not finish a job either but something about Whisper doesn't seem right. It's off somehow and I don't like that feeling.

"What do you want to do, Steele?" Knox asks. I sit on the edge of the bed, resting my head in my hands as I think about that.

"We have to stop hurting her. Someone is already doing that," I say not sure that I even hear myself saying it. I can't believe those words come out of my mouth.

"Are you kidding me?" I jerk my head up to look at Callan as he stands in front of me with his arms crossed over his chest.

"No. Look at her! What good is she to us if she's broken?" That's not what this is about. Forget us. Forget what we were told to do. This is about me not being able to control myself around her. This is about what my head is telling me is wrong and what I feel is right.

"Goddamn it! You're falling for her," Knox roars loudly. I don't acknowledge him. I don't need to. I'm close to my brothers, closer to them than anyone else in my life and they know me the same way I know them.

"Well that complicates things," Callan muses.

"No, it doesn't. Nothing changes. If she was planted, she was stuck here to weasel her way in, we're going to find out about it. Just not the way we have been."

"So, what are we going to do? Apologize for being assholes and buy her chocolates?" Callan hisses.

"Not exactly. You're going to do those things." His head snaps around to look at me like I've gone insane and maybe I have.

"What does that mean?"

"You're the one that's been nice to her. You're the one that she trusts most out of all of us. You have to be the one to get in with her." He shakes his head, a laugh escaping him.

"Not a chance in hell. Do you even realize the look you get when anyone else is near her? Huh?" He raises his eyebrows as Knox laughs.

"He's right. No way can you sit back and watch your little brother play house with that girl." He adds his two cents that no one asked for.

"Then what do we do?" I ask shoving myself off the bed. Resting my hands on my hips, I look between the two of them waiting for an answer when Knox chuckles.

"You keep her for yourself, man. No way are we getting in the middle of that," he says pointing at her.

"Like you didn't touch her already," I challenge him. Both of them.

"That's different. You didn't give a damn about her before."

"And I still don't."

"Keep telling yourself that," Callan says. I move toward him quickly, my fist balled at my side. Just as I'm about to swing, Knox steps in between us, shoving me back a step.

"We don't do this! We don't fight each other!" His words slam into my chest like a lead weight. He's right we don't. My head is a mess as I take a step back and run my hand through my hair.

"You're right. I just don't know what I'm doing anymore. How much more shit I can handle from Dad's crew," I say honestly. I've taken hit after hit from them over the last month and my body and mind are wearing thin.

"We need to watch our backs. We're getting sloppy with our searches," Callan states. I nod.

"Let's all calm down and think about this. Dad doesn't come over here. She can stay here." My head snaps around to look at Knox as if he's lost his mind.

"She can't stay with us!" Callan roars as I nod.

"Why not? We need to figure out who she really is and I'm going to assume it's her new foster daddy that's beating her to hell."

"Why would he? What the hell does Nathan Weatherly have to gain from that?" It doesn't make sense. I've never known him to be abusive before, but I suppose there's a lot people don't know about each other in this town.

"She can't stay. Not unless she asks to stay, got it?" I look between the two of them before they share a glance. They both nod agreeing with me which is a shock in itself. I thought they may fight me on this but I'm glad they aren't.

"What now? What do we do now?" Callan asks.

"You two go see what you can find out about Nathan. I'm going to wait here in case she wakes up." Knox and Callan share a look before laughing and walking out of my room. I turn and look at her, lying there peacefully in her sleep. As morbid as it sounds, she almost looks dead. Her lips are pale, her skin too. Whatever it is that haunts her from the past really scared the shit out of her tonight and that alone intrigues me. Kicking my shoes off, I slip under the blankets next to her, pulling her worn out body into mine. Her heat radiates into me, my chest tightening.

"I don't want you to do this. I don't want you fucking with my head, Whisper."

"I'm sorry," she whispers back.

11

———

WHISPER

I feel like I've been hit by a truck. My head pounds and my body aches. Everything comes back to me in a rush as I sit up in the bed. When I look down, I see I'm naked in a warm, plush bed. Glancing over there's a note with a glass of water and pills that says take these. I don't care what they are at this point as I reach over and grab them, popping them into my mouth before downing the water. My throats so dry it feels like I haven't drunk anything in a year. I pull the blankets off my body and throw my legs over the edge of the bed and stand. Testing to see how dizzy I am, I stumble a little to the first dresser I find and pull the drawer open. I don't see my clothes anywhere as I pull out a t-shirt. That's when the smell hits me. It's Steele's shirt. I bring it to my nose and inhale the clean scent before slipping it over my head.

The door is closed so I take the chance to snoop around a little. On the other dresser is a picture of him and his brothers. It looks like it was maybe taken after a football game. They have their arms over each other's shoulders and smiling with a trophy sitting on the ground in front of them. The sight makes me smile. They look so happy. Far from the assholes I've come to know. I reach up and run my fingers over a gold necklace that lies next to the picture before turning and walking to the door. I need my clothes; I need out of here. I don't know what time it is, and I don't really care as the smell of bacon hits my nose. I glance left and right noting the end of the hall and head toward the stairs. I can hear them down there talking as I walk down.

"Tonight's game is going to be killer," Callan says.

"Nothing we can't win," Steele adds. They are so confident in themselves and although I've never seen them play a game, I've seen them practice.

"That's for sure. You don't think he'll show up do you?" Callan asks. I wonder who it is he's talking about.

"Not a chance in hell," Steele growls.

"Can I have my clothes?" I ask as my feet hit the floor. All eyes come to meet mine, Steele's dragging up and down my body. I can feel the heat from here but it's not him that moves. It's Callan. He rushes toward me, placing a hand on my arm.

"You okay? Feeling okay? Did you take the medicine?" Everything comes out of him in a rush as Knox chuckles and Steele stares daggers.

"I'm fine. I took them. Thanks."

"Hungry? You're probably starving," he implies.

"I just want my clothes."

"They're in the washer. Sit down," Steele demands. I shake my head when Callan moves back and Steele stalks toward me. He reaches up, his hand wrapping around the back of my neck, pulling me closer to him. This is different. Strange.

"Don't make me force you, Whisper."

"That would be a change now wouldn't it?" I challenge him.

His lips slowly curl into one of the hottest smirks that I've ever seen.

"You like when I get rough with you?" he asks, his lips inching closer to mine. Why does he do this to me? Why does he make me feel like this? I don't have time to think about it. His lips press into mine before a growl rips from his throat. His tongue forces its way into my mouth, tangling with mine. The way he possessively holds my head in his hand, the way his tongue slips along mine—my head is spinning and not from my fall. When he finally pulls back, I'm breathless. He nods at Callan who grabs my hand and leads me to the stools in front of the counter. What the hell? I didn't even protest!

Steele moves back to the stove and continues to cook as Knox slides a glass of juice in front of me. I look up at him confused but he just nods toward it.

"What is all this? Why am I here?"

"You don't remember passing out?" Callan asks, looking concerned.

"Yeah, I remember that part but why am I here? Where is here?"

"It's our house," Steele answers plating the food. He moves around, grabbing silverware and setting plates in front of all of us.

"So why am I in your house?" I ask once more.

"Eat the food, Whisper." Steele's growls are growing more annoying by the second. I huff out a breath and shove the plate away from me, crossing my arms over my chest.

"This is bullshit! Give me my damn clothes!" I yell like a three-year-old that got her favorite blanket taken away. Steele's jaw clenches as he slowly stands from the stool and leaves the kitchen.

"You shouldn't keep pushing him like that. He's trying," Knox says scooting the plate back in front of me.

"Pushing him? You three have tormented me for a month! Do tell how I'm pushing him?"

"It's not that easy, Whisper," Callan says.

"That's for damn sure," I grumble and climb off the stool. With a quick glance around, I head for the door. I'm out it and down the steps glancing around, trying to figure out where the hell I am. I'm not ashamed to walk home in his shirt. I'm not afraid of what people might think. I take two steps before I'm grabbed and lifted into the air.

"What the hell is wrong with you?" Steele roars.

"Put me down! I need to go home," I scream as he walks back up the steps and into the house. Steele moves through the room dropping me back down on the same stool I just left. I start to get back up when Knox grabs my arm. His hand moves to my stomach as I suck in a breath. Steele has me placed so that I'm facing him not the counter. His hand comes to my thigh, slowly inching his way up. I gasp from feeling him touching me. Knox's hand slips under the front of the t-shirt, slowly slipping up until he has my nipple between his fingers. My eyes move from Knox to Steele as he moves higher.

"What are you doing?"

"Calming you down." Callan moves, coming to stand next to me. His hand comes up, threading through my hair as I keep my eyes locked with Steele's. As good as they all feel touching me, it's his touch that I want. Callan's lips caress my neck. I arch into Steele's touch, gasping for air. His finger dips inside of me and I nearly leap off the stool.

"Steele," I say his name breathlessly.

"Hmm?"

"Why?"

"Why what?" he asks, his voice a mask of hardness. He isn't letting anything show and that bothers me.

"Why all of them?" I moan once more when Callan sucks my flesh into his warm mouth.

"You don't want all of them touching you?" he asks, raising an eyebrow. It only takes one shake of my head. One little shake and he's ripping me off the stool and carrying me up the steps. He takes them two at a time as my body overheats. We're back in his room; he dumps me on the bed before ripping his clothes off. In seconds, he's between my thighs, thrusting into me. I gasp, digging my nails into his back, feeling the muscles as they flex. God, I didn't think it would feel this good.

"Fuck," he growls after he bites into my neck. I scream his name, my body tensing with each rough thrust of his hips. Steele grabs my leg, lifting it over his shoulder as he fucks me harder. He growls, sweat dripping down his temples before dropping onto me. I want to lick him, taste him but everything is happening too quickly. As fast as he started, I feel him swell inside of me. A rough thrust and a loud growl later, he pinches my nipple making us both come.

Steele rests his head on my shoulder as he catches his breath. I don't know what this was or why it happened. He's tormented me for weeks and now he's fucking me like his life depends on it. I want to ask but I'm afraid of what might happen if I do. Steele slowly pulls out of me, a groan rumbling past his lips as he moves. He climbs off the bed as I watch him, spotting the scratches that my nails made on his perfect back. His muscles flex and my mouth waters.

"You're going to eat. That isn't up for discussion,"

he says pulling his clothes back on. I slide up the bed taking the blanket with me.

"Why am I here?"

"Now isn't the time for questions, Whisper."

"When is the time?" I ask. He turns his heated stare to me.

"When I say it's time. Right now, you're going to clean up and come eat. Then, we're going to go to school." With that, he turns and walks out of the room leaving me once more to my own thoughts. Blowing out a breath, I climb out of bed and head into the in-suite bathroom and turn the shower on. As soon as I step in, I let the warmth wrap me in its embrace and pull my thoughts to something that doesn't involve Steele between my legs.

12

—————

STEELE

The day went by in a blur. Whisper took off as soon as we got to school. I don't blame her. I would have run too. Now that classes are over, me, Knox and Callan are warming up for our game tonight. I can't keep the thoughts of her away from my brain though. The way she felt under me. The way she took all my weight and never complained. The scratches that still linger on my back.

I throw the ball back to Callan when Coach walks up.

"I don't need to tell you this is an important game," he says. I nod my head knowing that already.

"Like every other one," I add.

"Keep up that attitude, Steele." I roll my eyes and catch the ball when Callan throws it back. Rolling my head, I crack my neck from side to side when I see Shane.

"Your girl is here," I call out to Callan. He looks to his left and sees her before dragging his gaze back to me. He flips me off as I laugh. Coach calls us into the locker room just as Shane walks toward us. Those two have a history. A fucked up one at that. Shit from our pasts, our families, caused Callan to step away from her. It broke a part of him, I could see it in his eyes.

We all file into the locker room as the coach begins to talk. I roll my shoulders, stretch my legs as I listen to the same speech I always hear. Shane strolls in, her recorder in hand. I huff out a laugh until I see who it is that's behind her. Anger flares in my chest. What the hell is she doing in here? Her eyes move over the guys, coming to rest on mine while I grind my teeth together. I jerk my head to the side letting her know I want her to go in the back, but she just smirks and flips me off. Knots form in my stomach before I move. Coach watches me but doesn't say shit when I grab Whisper by the arm and drag her into the back of the locker room. As soon as we are out of everyone's view, I slam her roughly against the wall.

"What the hell are you doing in here?" One hand stays wrapped around her throat, the other I shove down the front of her pants. She's wet already which doesn't surprise me.

"Helping with the paper," she says softly.

"Are you? Or you checking the guys out?" Yeah, there may be a bit of jealousy there. I claimed her ass, I was inside of her and now she's mine whether she likes it or not. No one will be touching her but me. Whisper reaches for my hand, jerking it from her jeans and pushing it away.

"I believe I'm free to do what I want, Steele."

"Is that what you think?" I lean in closer, closing the space between us as I squeeze her throat a little harder.

"I don't need to think. I know. You don't own me," she says gritting her teeth. I love watching her like this. That fire, that burn.

"You don't think so? Who was inside of you today? Whose cock was filling you, Whisper?" She grins a dark grin at me.

"Do you think you're the only cock that's been inside of me?

Don't flatter yourself, Alder." Slapping my hand away from her throat, she storms from the back room and out into the front. I follow her out, licking my fingers as her gaze finds mine. She's pissed. Just the way I like her.

"What the hell was that?" Knox asks when I take my spot next to him.

"Just having a little fun." He chuckles before we go back to listening to Ray talk. Same speech as always. Get the ball, throw it to me. I love football, I love the freedom it gives me but it's not my passion. Of course, I will play it through college because I enjoy it but when I graduate, so does football. I zone out, ignoring Ray and all his antics. He tries to get us all amped up for the games but we don't need it. At least me and my brothers don't. We know what we're doing and we're the best on the team. I watch Callan as his eyes drift back to Shane. I don't know why he doesn't talk to her. That shit was years ago and handled as far as the founding families go. She isn't one of us. Never will be, but she moved in and stayed in Rolling Springs and she doesn't seem to be going anywhere. I nudge Knox and nod toward our little brother when he laughs. Everyone turns to look at him before quickly turning back.

"The hell was that?" I chuckle lightly.

"He needs his cock sucked," Knox says.

"Agreed. Now to get him to talk to her again."

"Good luck with that."

"We should bring her to Intensity tonight." His head jerks in my direction.

"You bringing Whisper?"

"Yeah. She can dance. I think she'd like it. Maybe even open up a little more when it involves something she actually likes."

"Which isn't us." Knox laughs again. I nod my head and agree this time. She doesn't like us much; we've made sure of that. Once Ray is finished, we all stand in a huddle. We rally ourselves up and head out of the locker room to get this game going.

Out on the field is a different world. There're different feelings you get in the pit of your stomach. I can't explain it and I'm not sure I want to. This is a life outside of our normal but it's also a place that we're free. Free from our family legacy, free from our fates. Out here, we're just us.

The game starts and I see Tricia in her little cheerleading outfit. I wonder what the hell I ever saw in her. Aside from being pretty, she has nothing else going for her. She's annoying and clingy.

I take a long look at her before the ball is snapped. I run, dodging assholes left and right. My eyes are on the ball as it spirals toward me. Catching it, I turn and run. I can feel the man coming up behind me. Then I'm slammed into the ground. Back on my feet, my brother slaps a hand on my shoulder before we do it all over again. The crowd roars to life. They love when my brothers and I are in, which is a majority of the game.

When it's over, we won thirty-two to nothing. Tonight, we celebrate. As I head into the locker room, sweaty and high, I see her once more. She's talking to Falkner, one of our other players. That acid in my stomach coils and seeps into my pores. I'm twenty seconds from heading over there when she looks over at me. A sick smirk crosses her face before she flips me off once more.

"Damn, Steele. You pissed her off," Callan says slapping a hand on my back.

"Seems so. That'll all change later."

"She going?" he asks, looking all hopeful and shit.

"Yeah, she's going. She just doesn't know it yet."

13

———

WHISPER

Dinner was a bust. Like a busted lip bust. Nathan is a complete bastard when Debra isn't here. He stands there staring me down as I wipe my face on a napkin.

"You don't follow rules well, do you?" he snarls.

"Not usually," I reply with a snarky tone.

"You should. You'll learn." He steps toward me as I straighten my spine. He's told me his plans which I don't really understand.

"What do you want from me, Nathan? Caring parent was all a load of shit," I tell him.

"You're right. There are many things you don't know about this town, about the founding families. Secrets, lies, cover-ups. That's all there is around here."

"What does that have to do with me?" He smirks, raising his hand to my cheek. I flinch thinking he's going to hit me again, but he doesn't. Instead, he caresses my cheek, letting his fingers run over my flesh.

"I wish I could tell you the whole story. I wish it was all that easy but it isn't. Just know that you aren't who you think you are. You belong here," he hisses, his fingers digging into my cheek. I wince when someone knocks on the door. Nathan pulls away and spins to go answer it. I blow out a breath and wonder what the hell he's talking about when I hear him.

"You aren't allowed here!" Nathan roars.

"I'm allowed anywhere in this goddamn town." Steele's voice booms through the room. Intrigued by what the hell he's doing here; I walk toward the door to find him towering over Nathan. His eyes are dark, darker than I've ever seen them.

"What are you doing here?"

"We came to get you," Knox says as if his brother isn't standing there ready to punch a hole through Nathan's face.

"To go where?"

"Out. Go change," Callan says nodding toward my clothes. I look down at what I'm wearing before bringing my eyes back to his.

"I'm not going anywhere with you."

"That's right she isn't!" Nathan adds. I lick the blood from my lip when Steele looks over.

"You're bleeding."

"She fell," Nathan says quickly trying to cover his own ass. Prick.

"What happened to you?" Steele asks.

"I fell." Turning on my heel, I hear the growl leave him. That stops me in my tracks. It's feral and unhinged. I turn back just in time to see him ball his fists. I move quickly, grabbing his arm and pulling as hard as I can until he follows me. I lead him up the stairs and down the hall as Knox and Callan laugh. As soon as we're in my room, I spin around to face him.

"What the hell is with you? Huh? You can't go around beating on my foster family!"

"He hit you, Whisper!"

"You don't know what you're talking about!" Anger creeps into my veins. I don't need his help. Why doesn't he understand that? Why can't he see that I'm fine on my own?

"He has no right to touch you," he growls.

"And you do?" I ask cocking my head to the side to look up at him. His eyes dance between mine before he grabs my face roughly in his hands. His lips crash into mine causing me to wince. The heat in his kiss, the demand—it's all so much. It all feels right when it's all so wrong.

"You. Are. Mine."

"No, I'm not. I'm nobody's. I never will be. Now what are you doing here?" I ask once more, slapping his hands away from me.

"We're going out. Somewhere I think you'll like," he says causally as if this little showdown didn't just happen. He's so hot and cold. I never know what version of Steele I'm going to get and I kind of like that.

"I'm not going." Crossing my arms over my chest, he grins darkly.

"You don't come, and I will go down those stairs and beat that asshole until he can't remember his own name." I watch him, gauging him. I have no doubt he'll do it. I saw him beat that man to death that night. I wasn't supposed to be there but I saw it.

"Why?"

"Why what?"

"Why would you beat him? I don't mean anything to you, Steele."

"You don't know shit," he hisses stepping closer. I can't do this with him tonight. I've already had enough shit with Nathan.

"Fine. I'll go." He nods his head and steps back while I grab my clothes. I grab my loose-fitting jeans, a white tank top and my yellow jacket before stripping. Fuck, Steele. I don't care what he sees anymore. As soon as my clothes hit the floor, he growls. I know there're new bruises. I know that he now knows Nathan put them there but after his threats, I can't say a word. I won't go to jail and I sure as hell won't give up dancing. I don't know if Nathan would really do it or not considering he wants something more from me, but I don't want to take the chance. I pull my boots on and grab a hair tie, piling my hair up on top of my head before turning to face Steele. Holding my arms out wide I say, "Happy now?"

"Not even a little. Let's go." Moody Steele is back as I grab my phone and slide it into my pocket. Heading out into the hall-way, Steele grabs my arm and pulls me back a step. His eyes search mine, a softness crossing his features.

"I'm okay, Steele." He doesn't move for another long second. The muscle in his jaw works as I watch him, really looking into his eyes. Finally, he nods his head and I pull my arm free, heading down the stairs.

"Let's go," I snap as if I'm not happy they're here. I mean, to be fair I'm not really sure how I feel with them showing up here. I'm torn. I want to like them, but I also know what they do to people, what they did to me.

"Don't stay out late!" Nathan snaps behind me as I head out the door. I flip him off when I hear Callan.

"She might not be home tonight, Dad, and you will accept that." With that we all pile into the SUV as I smirk at Nathan's face out the window. Thank God they are tinted, and he can't see me.

"Where are you taking me, kidnappers?" I ask sarcastically. Callan shifts so he's looking at me while Steele drives and Knox fills the front seat.

"You love dancing, don't you?" I swallow hard, not knowing where this conversation is going to take me. I see Steele out of the corner of my eye watching me in the rearview mirror.

"It's the only thing that calms me. It keeps me sane," I admit. Callan smiles and nods his head.

"I could see that when you were in class."

"You watched me?"

"Everyone's watched you, Whisper," Knox chimes in. A rumble sounds from Steele as I shake my head and look back to Callan.

"Why were you watching me?"

He shrugs. "I don't know. There's something alluring about you when you dance. I don't know that you see it in yourself," he says. The sincerity in his tone is what slams into my chest. He means it. He sees something more in me when I dance.

"I don't know what to say," I admit. Callan chuckles and reaches over, pulling me into his side.

"A small thank you is fine. Not everything has to be complicated between us, Whisper." What the hell does that even mean?

"Thank you, Callan."

"You two girls done sharing feelings back there?" Callan laughs as Steele gets even more aggravated. He reaches for the radio, turning the music up louder.

"You also sing like an angel," Callan whispers in my ear. I find myself resting my head on his shoulder as I belt out the words to the Pink song that's playing. The rest of the ride is pretty uneventful.

14

STEELE

I rest my hand on the small of her back as I lead her to the front of the line. Whisper's eyes move over the building and all the people that are lined up to get in, not saying a word. When we reach the door, the bouncer, Mitch smiles and waves us in.

"What is this place?" Whisper asks looking up at me. I just smirk and keep her walking. People slap their hands on our backs and shoulders as we make our way into the room. Intensity isn't your normal dance club. This is for *the* dancers. The ones that know how to move and want to show off. Of course, we still have some regular nights here but tonight isn't one of them. Tonight, I want to get into Whisper's head. Tonight is all about her and learning her. She gasps and comes to a complete stop when we reach the middle of the room. The music is loud, bass bumping.

"Oh, my God," she breathes as she looks up at me. Her eyes water with unshed tears when I shake my head. I reach up and wipe the lone tear away before leaning down.

"Don't do that. This is your night," I whisper in her ear. Whisper swallows hard and grabs my face in her hands. At first, I think she's going to kiss me but she doesn't. She just stares at me as if I'm a fucking mirage. When she releases me and turns back to the center of the room, I spot Leddy. She's one of the best female dancers we know. If anyone will give Whisper a run, it'll be her. I watch her move, the way her body flexes and shifts. Leddy is something else. She's gorgeous as hell but she also knows how to use her body to get what she wants. Whisper notices where my gaze is, and I don't miss the way her body tenses. I should reassure her that I want between her thighs not Leddy's, but I don't. Instead, I track Leddy's movements letting Whisper think whatever it is she wants to.

When Leddy is passed the mic, her eyes find mine. I smile and pop my head at her as I watch the smile pull across her face. Whisper tenses even more before turning and trying to walk away. I don't let her get that far. My hand comes to rest on her stomach as Leddy talks.

"Ya'll are in for a treat tonight! Not only is it Hot Mix night, we also have the Alder boys in the house!" The crowd goes insane hearing our name.

"Also, we have a new girl in the house! From what I hear she is quite the dancer. Tonight, we will get a chance to see her in action. Let's give Whisper a hot as fuck Intensity welcome!" Whisper's eyes jerk to mine and hold there. I can't tell if she's happy or pissed. Either way, it's going to be a fun night.

"Shut up! Now you know the rules, but Whisper doesn't. So let's break them down for her. You get three minutes all to yourself, but you have to pick a partner. Ladies' choice of course! We want to see what you got for those three minutes and show us just how sweaty you can make your partner get!" Leddy is hyped up for this. I knew she would be when I first called and told her

Whisper was coming with us tonight. The crowd is even wilder, larger than a normal night too.

"What did you do?" Whisper screams over the roar of the crowd at me.

"Let it go, Whisper. Show them what you're made of." It's a taunt. It's a challenge and I want to see if she has the balls to own up to it. This shift in power between us is unsettling. I don't like it and I don't like the way I feel around her. I've never given a shit about anyone and now Whisper is stepping all over that. I find myself torn between hating her and wanting her all to myself.

"Let's do it, Whisper! Pick your partner!" The beat starts to drop. UgeneUs featuring Antonia Marquee remix "Here We Go Again" starts thumping through the speakers. Whisper smiles up at me and I give her a sexy smile back. She reaches her hand out and I almost move to take it when she grabs Knox instead. The crowd roars as she drags him into the middle of the room. My jaw flexes as I keep my eyes on her. I should have known she would pull something like this.

She starts to move and it's fucking hypnotic. Her body flows to the music, each twist and turn perfectly performed. Knox stands still watching her when she moves closer. Wrapping her arms around his neck, she rolls her body against his. The movements get cheers and praise from all around. Knox bites his bottom lip and keeps his eyes on hers. Whisper gives him a show. She gives him a dance that should be all mine. When she turns and drops to the floor in front of him, I clench my fists. Callan is cheering her on as I'm about to explode.

"You did this!" he hollers over the music to remind me. Cracking my neck from side to side I watch as she arches her back, dragging that perfect ass up the front of my brother. Then the music changes and I move. Shoving Knox back, I grab Whisper around the back of her neck and pull her close to me.

"Dance for me." Those words were all she needed to hear. Rhianna's "Umbrella" remix plays now. Grabbing her hips, I spin her to face away from me. Shoving her back, she bends over, her ass pressing into my cock as the crowd screams.

"Oh, we have some competition!" Leddy screams into the mic. I tune her out, pulling Whisper into me. She moves her hips, pops them and holds before jerking her back and doing it all over again.

We get into a steady rhythm, the two of us moving around the floor as if we've danced together our whole lives. Sweat drips down her temples but the look on her face is pure enjoyment. She's relaxed and calm. Her head isn't in the bad space that she always seems to be in. She's free. On this dancefloor, Whisper is free.

She spins, wrapping her arms around my neck, pressing her body into mine. Her lips hover mere inches away from mine and just as I lean in to press my lips to hers, she moves. Her body rolls, pressing herself to mine before spinning around. Her back pressed to my front, she slides down my body and bends over. Her hips are in my hands as she grinds against me. When she's standing upright, I grab her hand and spin her out away from my body before jerking her back in. Her eyes light up as laughter falls from her lips. I don't think I've ever seen her like this before. I'm not sure she's ever seen herself like this before.

"Come on, Whisper!" Leddy yells, pulling her away from me. Whisper goes happily when Knox grabs my arm and tugs me toward the bar. I order a few drinks and turn to watch them together.

"She's fucking hot as hell," Knox announces.

"No shit." I bring my beer to my lips as I take her in. I can't believe that she is out there this freely with people she's never met. This is where she belongs. She belongs on a dancefloor somewhere. Music videos, choreographer training. That's what she's meant to do. I wonder if she's ever thought about it? Shaking my head, I need to focus. I need to focus on the job and not on her. This is fucking with my head and seeing her grind against Leddy is fucking with my cock.

"You brought her here," Callan reminds me when he grabs the beer from my hand. I shake my head and scrub my hand over my face wondering if this was the best decision I've ever made or the worst. I don't answer him, just nod my head. A few girls come up to us trying to get us to dance but I wave them off. My eyes are zoned in on her. I can't stop looking at her. She's so damn energetic and magnetic. Every man in the room, hell every woman in the room is watching her. I don't think there's a pair of eyes that aren't on her. Something in my chest tightens.

"You good?" Knox asks leaning into me.

"Yeah, why?" I don't look away. I can't.

"Your grinding your teeth until they're about to break, man."

"No, I'm not."

"Just go get her, Steele." I ignore him for about half a second when I see another guy moving in behind her. That's when I lose it. I storm through the room, grabbing her by the hips and jerking her back into my body. She doesn't protest, she just keeps moving as if nothing can hurt her.

Like I can't hurt her.

WHISPER

"You don't have to act like you didn't have a good time," Callan says as I watch Steele. Knox is driving, Callan is in the passenger seat spun around so he can look at me, but I can't take my eyes off Steele. The way he held me, touched me. It was more than just a dance and I craved it. I wanted it more than anything else in the world. I've never felt that kind of raw connection to anyone and I've danced my whole life. With Steele, it was natural. It wasn't forced and that is pissing me off. The man that's tormented me over the last month had a hold on me in that building and I couldn't break it.

"Stop fucking staring at me," he says looking out his window.

"How did you do it?"

"Do what?"

"Make me feel like that." Callan chuckles but I ignore him. He didn't feel it. He couldn't have. Steele doesn't look my way and that angers me further.

"Did you have fun, Whisper?" Knox asks from his spot in the front.

"Tell me!" I scream until Steele looks over.

"I don't know what you're talking about." The look in his eyes tells me he's lying. He's sitting there lying to me and I don't know why.

"Dance… when you dance with someone, there's no way to describe what you feel. When you connect… it's like the whole damn universe is aligned and everything is right. I've never in my whole life felt that," I admit softly. Knox lets out a low whistle, Callan curses under his breath but Steele? He stares at me as if I've lost my mind. He had to have felt it. The way he moved with me, touched me. That kind of connection is on a deeper level than sex.

"I don't know what the hell you were feeling but that's not what it was," Steele says through gritted teeth.

"You're going to sit there and lie about it? You took me there and now you lie?" I yell loudly. Steele shifts in his seat so that he's fully facing me now.

"You felt hot and horny. You're attracted to me, Whisper. Don't overthink that. We can fuck and we have chemistry to do it but don't go overthinking that." Air leaves my lungs in a rush as I listen to his words. Harsh and cruel and all fucking lies. I can see the way he looks at me. I can tell by the way he touches me but if this is the game he wants to play, I will gladly play along.

"You're right," I say under my breath. I sit in silence the rest of the ride back to their place. As soon as we're out of the car, Callan has his arm around my shoulders.

"What's your favorite drink?" Looking up at him, I know where this is headed, and I gladly accept it after that blow from Steele in the car.

"Whiskey. All kinds." He nods as we all head into the house.

I strip out of my jacket and toss it onto the chair while Callan moves into the kitchen.

"What do you feel when you're out there?" Knox asks leaning against the counter as he stares at me.

"There's no way to describe it. It's freeing. I'm weightless." His lips curl into a smile that could break any female.

"You looked it. Free, I mean. You always keep a mask in place at school but tonight… I saw that mask slip for just a little while. The real Whisper showed through and that one? Is far sexier and free than the one we usually get."

"What do you expect from me when all you three do is make my life hell? You want a smile? A thank you?" Knox shakes his head as anger fuels me.

"It isn't what you think, Whisper."

"Nothing is! Not you three, not the Weatherly's! Everyone wants something from me, so why don't we stop with the games and you tell me what that is." Callan thrusts a glass into my hand and I swallow it down quickly. He replaces it with another before heading back to the counter.

"I think we should at least talk about it with her," Callan says with his back to me.

"About what?" I ask.

"Don't do this shit! We have rules for a reason, Callan!" There's Steele. He disappeared for a minute and when I spin around to look at him, I see he's changed. He stands there, his perfectly sculpted chest on full display. My eyes drag down to the V that disappears into his gym shorts. Fuck, why is he doing this to me? Tossing back the next drink, I shove the glass at Callan and motion for another. He chuckles and refills it.

"What reasons? Why can't I know what the hell is going on around here?" I scream. The guys all shift but Steele? That bastard holds my stare, daring me.

"It's dangerous," he says as if it's nothing.

"You're dangerous." That was my reply.

"That's not untrue. You're just as dangerous if you are who we think you are," he responds.

"Who the hell do you think I am? I'm Whisper Jane Sullens! The girl nobody wants. I'm the dancer in the dark, the girl that's overlooked because she isn't worth looking at!" Okay maybe the alcohol is doing a little talking here but deep down that's what I feel.

"What? That's the most ridiculous thing I've ever heard," Knox says.

"Is it? I was never adopted. What is so wrong with me?" I yell looking between them. They share a glance, but they let me have my meltdown. I don't want to. I don't want them to see me lose control but at the same time I'm tired of holding on. Tired of holding it in.

"What? Huh? Was it because I wasn't the blonde hair blue-eyed baby the other girls were? Is it because I'm used and broken? The fact that I have scars that run deeper than the fucking ocean inside my heart? What is it? What is wrong with me?" Tears spring from my eyes as I drop to the floor crying into my hands. This was a mistake. I shouldn't be here talking to them.

"Get up." The demand in his tone does nothing for me. Fuck Steele. I keep sobbing into my hands when he roars louder, "Get. Up." Lifting my head, I see him playing on his phone. In seconds, Usher and Beyoncé remix of "In This Club" sounds all around us. Steele hardens himself before moving to pull a chair out in the middle of the floor.

"Dance for me," he demands. I shake my head, but he just raises an eyebrow in challenge. The music, the tempo, slowly makes its way into my body, pumping through my veins. I slowly stand up, letting my body roll with the music. His eyes are glued to my body. The heat in them causes me to shiver. I've never been watched the way he's watching me.

"Dance, Whisper." Only then do I realize that I stopped and stared back at him. I close my eyes, raise my arms above my head and slowly sway. Once I'm into a good groove, I really start moving. Spinning, dropping to the floor, I crawl toward him before grabbing his knees and pulling myself back up. Tipping my head back, I reach up and pull the tie from my hair and let my hair fall down my back. Shaking my hair out, I flip my head forward and lock eyes with him. I run my fingers through my hair while I straddle his lap. My body arches, twists, and presses into his. I can feel just how hard he is, and it makes me smile slightly. Steele's hands come up quickly, grabbing my face in his strong hands. Alcohol courses through my veins, begging me to do something I know I shouldn't be.

"You aren't nobody. There is nothing wrong with you. You're… goddamn it, Whisper, you're perfect!" he growls before crashing his lips against mine. His grip has me gasping for air. His kiss is fierce when I hear the other two laughing. Footsteps sound behind us but I'm lost in Steele. I'm lost in his touch, his warmth, in his darkness.

He lifts me in his arms and I automatically wrap my legs around his waist as the song repeats. Sparks ignite inside of me as he moves to slam my body on the table. I gasp into his mouth as he grinds himself against me. There's a slight restraint inside of me. I know that if I give in to him right now, things are going to change. I can feel it in the air, the way it crackles and sizzles around us.

"I got you, Whisper," he says as he sits up and pulls my clothes off in record time. My boots thud to the floor followed by my jeans and shirt. His lips caress my stomach as he kisses and licks my flesh. I arch into him, loving the way my body vibrates when he touches me. I close my eyes as his teeth skim my neck. Then he's back, kissing me so deeply that my body begs to be taken. His hand shifts down my side before moving between us. His cock is hard and ready as he slowly slips into me. I gasp from the size of him, feeling him inside of me. He's lucky I'm on birth control or I'd have to halt our fun. Steele doesn't seem to care either way as he groans into my neck. His tongue swipes out, licking my earlobe.

"What the hell are you doing to me, Whisper?" he murmurs so softly, I almost miss it. His hips slowly rock into me and everything I've been holding back, slowly comes to the surface as I ride the high that Steele gives me.

16

STEELE

I run my fingers through her dark hair as she traces the lines of my muscles on my stomach. There's been a strange silence lingering between the two of us since I brought her back up to my room. There're so many things that I want to say to her but none of them come out. I don't know what I'm doing with her. I want to hate her, hate what she's caused yet I don't think I can.

"I was five. I've always wanted to dance; it didn't matter what kind of dancing either. My foster mom gave me an old ballerina costume," she says swallowing hard. I don't stop moving my fingers through her hair. "I remember dancing in the living room. Tony, my foster dad hated it when I'd come in there. He would yell at me, scream until he was hoarse. Then one day, he grabbed me. Drug me to my room and ripped the stained tutu off me. The leggings, I remember how dirty they were when I got them, torn knees. I didn't care, you know? I just wanted to dance and be free. I cried when he ripped that old tutu to shreds."

"What did he do, Whisper?"

"He leaned down, covered my mouth with his hand and told me if I ever told anyone or screamed, he would make sure I never danced again. Then he molested me."

"Fuck," I growl tightening my hand in her hair.

"Gang-raped. I couldn't believe how much I actually liked what you guys did to me when that thought has always sat in the back of my mind."

"How old were you?"

"Thirteen."

"Dammnit, Whisper!" I'm pissed. No, pissed isn't what I'm feeling. Murderous. I want to murder anyone that has ever put their hands on her.

"I don't feel bad for what we did." It may be a dick move but I don't care. I don't regret it even after what she just said to me. She giggles a little and keeps her fingers moving.

"Didn't want you to be. Nathan, he's said similar things to me. How he could make it so I couldn't dance again. That's the only thing I have left in me, Steele. I can't let him take that away from me."

"What's he want from you?" I'm not so sure that I want the answer to that, but I have to know what I'm up against with her.

"I'm not sure honestly. He's very cryptic with what he says. He keeps telling me that I belong here and that it will all come to light. He wants me to give him information on you guys." My hand stills and so does hers. I take a few deep breaths before shifting so she has to move off me.

"What have you told him?" I growl. She watches me, her eyes narrowed as she does. She licks her lips then smiles.

"Wouldn't you like to know?" She climbs out of the bed and grabs my shirt, tugging it over her head before heading toward the door.

"Where the hell do you think you're going?" The anger that

laces my voice isn't really at her but in a way it is. She still isn't being open with me. She spins around, her hands on her hips.

"I just gave you a piece of me, Steele. Don't ask for all of it at once." With that she walks out of my room slamming the door behind her. I suck air through my nose before climbing out of bed and grabbing my shorts. I don't want her to leave, not yet. And I sure as hell don't want her anywhere near Nathan until I can figure out what the hell is going on. Storming into the hallway, I'm down the stairs only to find her sitting at the counter with Callan. She turns her head toward me, not a hint of a smile on her face before looking back to him.

"So, Intensity. Halloween Bash, you in?" Callan asks her. Her smile lights up the goddamn room as she nods her head.

"What's the theme? Are we getting matching costumes?" she teases.

"That depends, you want to be jelly? I'll be peanut butter?" he asks. She laughs and that right there is the best sound I've ever heard. Why I'm so drawn to Whisper is a mystery to me. To anyone else, she is probably just another girl, but to me, she's everything. What the hell is wrong with me? I turn around when I hear Knox stomping down the steps.

"Dad called." My arms immediately cross over my chest as I glare at him.

"And?"

"And he wants to see us," he says not sounding at all happy about it.

"About what?" I know the answer before I even ask but I still need the confirmation. His eyes slowly drag to Whisper even though she isn't paying attention to us. She's still laughing with Callan.

"This isn't going to end well," Knox says looking back at me.

"I know that."

"What are you going to do?" he asks. Ultimately this is all up to me. No matter what I choose someone is going to get hurt. The thought had crossed my mind more than once but now that Dad knows we've been around her, or that I've been fucking her for that matter, shit is going to fly. The question is, am I going to toss her ass to the side and continue with our mission or take what he has to offer and keep her? Scrubbing my hand over my face, I look back over at her before shaking my head and turning on my heel. I quickly climb the stairs and head back into my room. Closing the door, I clench my eyes shut and restrain from punching the wall. Instead, I go into my bathroom, turn the water to the shower on and stare at myself in the mirror.

My entire life has revolved around being the man that my dad wanted me to be. Doing his dirty work and to a point I love it. I've thrived on being who I am. The founding families of this place, of Rolling Springs are twisted and warped. They're people that normal people wouldn't want to mess with because they have the power to bring you to your knees. I've always known that playing against the rules would land me in trouble. I just never expected it to be a girl. A girl that I was supposed to break. A girl that could turn out to be the most powerful person in Rolling Springs. That thought alone pisses me off more than it should.

The door opens slowly and she walks in, pulling the shirt over her head and tossing it to the floor. Without another word, she walks past me, grabbing my hand on the way and pulling me toward the shower. We both step in and the heat hits me. She spins around, pressing her hands to my chest as I lower my head to look her in the eyes.

"Something I've learned a long time ago is, you can't choose your fate. It's always been written in the blood that covers your hands. It doesn't matter how hard you want to change it, you are who you are and who you were meant to be. No one can change that for you." Her words don't settle me. In fact, they piss me off more because I know my fate isn't a part of hers. This life, these people, they will suck you dry and leave you for dead if you don't follow their rules.

"Fates change," I tell her, watching her as her hands slide over my chest and down to my cock. She grabs it in her hand, slowly stroking it as she shakes her head.

"No, they don't. In the end, fate always wins. We're born to be something, to do something, and that's just God's plan for us. We don't have the power to change it so whatever it is you're thinking about me and you, don't. There's a connection, that part is undeniable, but we aren't fated to be together, Steele. We're merely two dancers on the same stage but we will never share the spotlight."

17

WHISPER

"I heard you were sexy as hell at Intensity the other night," Shane says as we walk down the hall. I've avoided the Alder boys the last few days in search of what I need to know.

"Yeah, it was hot. Are you going to the Halloween Bash?" Shane shrugs but then looks to me.

"Is Callan going?"

"Yeah. Why?"

"Then I probably won't." Annoyed with her whiny shit, I turn to walk backwards and stop in front of her.

"You know what, I like you Shane. You are probably one of the most down-to-earth people that I've met here but this shit is annoying. You want him. You love him, so stop being such a goddamn baby and go after him. I don't care what happened in the past between you two and frankly it's not my business. Be who you are meant to be, Shane." Her mouth falls open as I spin around and walk away. I hurry through the halls and into the library before I can be seen. I need more information than what anyone is giving me. All I've heard is that I'm supposed to be here. I don't know what the hell that means but I intend to find out.

I stopped and asked the librarian where I could find books on the history of Rolling Springs. She happily directed me, but she's been lingering close by ever since.

I've read through page after page about anything and everything. The founding families are the Alder's, the Macron's and the McLean's. From what I can find, the Weatherly's married into the Macron family but were later run out of town because they didn't stick to the rules which are still vague. I search and search until my eyes cross and I drop my head onto the table in front of me.

"What are looking for?" I snap my head up at the woman's voice only to realize it's the librarian.

"Uh, just looking." She fingers the books and glances around before sitting across from me.

"The Alder's basically run this town. McLean is the mayor but that doesn't really mean much. The McLean family was second to come to Rolling Springs. They made a place here, a home. The Alder's accepted that because they needed to branch out into the world. Their sole properties, houses, businesses were here and eventually those would fill up. They were smart, the older Alder's. They allowed the Macron family to come into their world based solely on the fact that they were from old money. Their connections ran deep."

"And the Weatherly's?" I ask curious to know more.

"Ah, the Weatherly's married into the Macron's. Long ago one of the men fell for the lovely Weatherly. Nancy was her name. She was a nobody. Not of wealth, not of their class. The McLean's let it happen, but the Alder's and the Macron's didn't agree. They despised her and that turned into a war. A war that ended in blood and the Weatherly's being removed from Rolling Springs," she says. I'm so confused.

"So, Rolling Springs is all about money?" She smiles and glances around once more.

"Rolling Springs was built on money and darkness. The Alder's own many billion-dollar companies. They dip into everything from aviation to banking. Their reach is far and their money is powerful, but with power comes the dark side of things. Once you cross them, you aren't safe."

"Do you know who I am?" I blurt the question out without second guessing it.

"You're stepping into a world that I'm not sure you're ready for. If you were smart, you'd walk away now."

"I can't," I whisper, thinking of what Nathan had said, what Steele had said.

"I know. The Macron family… they had ties to people outside of Rolling Springs, other families. Their main goal was to take over Rolling Springs forcing the Alder family out."

"What? How could they do that?" She shrugs.

"They had more pull, more money, more alliances. Carson Macron was a force to be reckoned with. He was powerful in his own right. There's fear in the founding families. Fear that if just one Macron returns to Rolling Springs that the Alder's will lose everything, including control of the town."

"Why? What does one Macron have to do with anything? Surely they can fight one." She smiles and shakes her head.

"This particular Macron isn't just a Macron. She's also a McLean. Which in turn makes her stronger than any other family here." It all hits me, making me dizzy.

"Am… oh, my God."

"Welcome to the world, Whisper Macron." My heart leaps

into my throat. She begins to stand when I reach out and grab her wrist.

"How do you know me?" Straightening her spine, she holds her head high and smiles.

"We're half-sisters, Whisper. We share a father, although I was left as much as you were. I found my way back here many years ago under a new name, a new identity. I haven't been found out yet and I'd appreciate it if it stayed that way," she says, her tone turning cold. A sister? I have a sister?

"Why would you want to come back?"

"I don't know how to answer that, Whisper. I never belonged anywhere else. I'm Crystal, by the way."

"Why? Why were we dumped?"

"Don't you get it? Don't you listen?" she hisses, leaning down into my space. "We are nothing! We are bred between two of the most hated families in Rolling Springs, Whisper!" I open my mouth to say more but there is nothing. Everything I thought I knew about myself, my life, it's all lies. It's all fucking lies and now I'm being used by the ones I trusted, if only slightly. Closing the books, I stand and pick them up, passing them back to Crystal.

"No one will find out anything. Would you mind putting these back?" I ask her. She takes the books from my hands as I shrug my backpack over my shoulder and walk toward the door.

Who the hell do they think they are? They want to play games with me, I can play them just as well. They think they can break me? Let's see how they like it when the tables are turned.

18

———

STEELE

I'm afraid of what my dad has to say. I'm afraid of what might be happening now. We've kept him out of the loop and as far as he knows, we were still looking into things with Whisper. I can only imagine that he has heard more. It's not like I was hiding the fact that I was with her.

"Where's your head at, Steele?" Ray growls after I missed the last pass. I can't think straight. My head is a complete mess with what might be going on and the words that Whisper said in the shower have burned deeply inside of me. They stung but she's right. We will never be in the spotlight together because she's better off on her own.

"Why don't you go out there and play?" I roar before heading back onto the field. We run the play and when I'm hit, I get pissed. Pulling my helmet off, I storm at the other player. The crowd is screaming and so is the coach. Knox appears in front of me, shoving me back a step but I just brush him off and keep going. Grabbing the other guy by the front of his jersey, I'm ready to rip his head off. This isn't the first time this game that

I've gone off either. The ref comes over, waving his hands before I'm being grabbed and pulled back.

"You're out, Alder!" he calls out. I flip him off, grab my helmet and storm off the field. No one follows me and I'm glad for that. Callan and Knox need to stay in and play if we're going to win this one. As soon as I'm in the locker room, Shane appears.

"Care to make a statement?" she teases.

"Fuck off, Shane. Get the hell out of here." I sneer. She takes a step back when I say more, "It wasn't your fault you know?"

"What are you talking about?"

"You and Callan. He was doing what he was told to do. He didn't want to hurt you." What the hell am I doing? Digging myself deeper into the dark is what I'm doing. I'm fucking myself over and I only have her to blame. Fucking Whisper!

"I don't care. He could have stood up to your dad, Steele. He didn't have to hurt me in the process," she snaps.

"Like hell he didn't. If you believe that than you are stupider than I thought!"

"Go to hell, Steele. All of you! You all have choices!" I don't mean to react, I just do. I have her pinned against the wall in seconds, breathing heavily.

"Let her go," I hear Whisper call out. I grin at Shane before slowly releasing the hold I have on her. She doesn't move, just stands there in shock of what I've just done to her. All the while, Whisper comes closer. I pull my pads and jersey off, tossing them onto the floor when she steps in front of me.

"What the hell is that about?" I want to snap at her too. I want to slam her against the wall and fuck her until she admits to being mine, but I can't.

"Questions. It's always about the questions isn't it?" I ask, watching her closely.

"If you have something to ask me, Steele, just ask." She's different. Something is different with her, I can see it in her eyes.

"Where have you been the last few days?" I don't know why I'm asking. I don't know why I care. When that little smile tugs across her face, I can feel the air around us shift.

"Shane, you can go," she says, dismissing her friend like she was never meant to be here. Shane hurries off out of the locker room, but my eyes stay locked with Whisper's. "I thought we needed a little break from each other," she adds.

"A break? Why?"

"Why not? Things were getting too heated, Steele. Too complicated," she tells me. The only thing complicated is her.

"Is that right? So you ran from me?"

"No, it wasn't like that. I'm here, aren't I? I needed space. I needed to figure things out," she admits.

"What things?" She sighs and runs her hand through her long dark hair as she thinks over what she's about to say.

"Things Nathan said to me didn't make a lot of sense. When he'd mention things…" she trails off.

"Like what?"

"Do you know who I am, Steele? Like who I really am?" There it is. The question that I knew would come at some point.

"You don't understand what's happening here, Whisper." She steps into my space, grabbing me around the neck and pulling my lips to hers. I let her kiss me. I let her take whatever kind of aggression she has in her out on me because after this, I don't know what's going to happen.

"I want you, Steele," she whispers against my lips. I lift her easily, she wraps her legs around my waist. Carrying her into the back where the showers are, I let her fall to her feet. She watches me while she pulls her jeans off and kicks her shoes to the side. I wriggle out of my game pants and pull my boxers down before moving toward her. She doesn't say a word as I lift her effortlessly and slide into her. She gasps, clinging to me like her life depends on it. Holding her hips in my hands, I pump into her. Whisper pants as I fuck her against the shower wall. Neither of us say a word and that's probably for the best. Each thrust feels like it's the last. Something is morphing between us, pulling us apart and I'm not sure I'm ready to deal with that.

Her nails dig into my shoulders as I feel her pussy clench around me.

"Steele," she moans as I come apart inside of her. She clenches again and I feel her walls constrict around me as she gasps for air. Her whimpers will forever be burned into my memory.

"I know who you are," I whisper in her ear before biting her earlobe. Once again, she clamps down around me and moans.

"Who am I?" she asks breathlessly.

"Whisper Macron." Her body tenses as I slowly pull out of her and let her feet fall to the floor.

"How did you find out?" she asks, looking up at me as I grab my boxers and head toward my locker to grab my clothes. She follows behind me, her clothes in her hand.

"I'm not some stupid jock, Whisper."

"I know that," she snaps as she pulls her jeans and shoes back on. "So what are you going to do about it?" I look over at her as I pull my clothes on before sitting on the bench to put my shoes on.

"That's the thing, I don't know. If my dad finds out, he will order us to kill you."

"He has to know," she adds.

"No, that was our job. We were supposed to find out. How long have you known?" I'm curious now. Not that it makes a difference to me, I don't plan on letting her walk away as easily as she thinks she can.

"Not long."

"What are your plans now that you know?" I ask grabbing my bag and throwing it over my shoulder. I motion for her to follow me when all I really want to do is snap her goddamn neck for avoiding me and fucking with my head. Either way, she follows me out to the SUV and climbs in the passenger seat. Once I toss my bag in the back and settle in, I glance over at her.

"What am I supposed to do? No one wants me. It's pretty clear that my family shit on me when I was born and threw me away. They never wanted me." There's a hint of sadness in her tone that bothers me. Whisper has nothing to be sad about. She just learned who she truly is. That in itself should have her smiling and jumping with joy.

"You couldn't be here," I finally admit. While she's been searching, so have I. I didn't want to tell her the truth until I had every piece of this fucked up puzzle in my hands, but I can't keep this from her either.

"What do you mean?" Now I have her attention.

"You weren't just a Macron, Whisper."

"I know, I'm a McLean too." I chuckle at how she says it. Like it means nothing.

"You don't get it do you? The power of both of those families could tear this town apart, Whisper."

"Except for the small fact that they didn't want me!"

"The affair was fucked up. In this world, affairs happen but bringing a child is never accepted. They had to get rid of you or they would have all lost their places." Not that it makes it any better but that's the truth.

"This is all stupid. It's all bullshit," she says, sounding completely over all of it already and it hasn't even begun. I slip my hand across the seat and grab hers in mine before taking a deep breath and blowing it out.

"Shit's going to get a little more complicated," I warn her.

"Why? What more could there possibly be?" Her eyes meet mine and a slow dark smile pulls across my face.

"My dad."

19

WHISPER

My knee bounces as I sit in the seat next to Callan and Knox. I don't know what's happening here. I don't know why I am supposed to be here, but in the middle of the room is an octagon ring that looks like something out of the MMA. My stomach churns and rumbles as I wait.

"Why am I here?" I ask looking up at Knox.

"You'll see." His jaw tics and I know that's a sign that something is wrong. No one will inform me of what that is though.

"This is bullshit. I'm leaving," I snap, shoving out of my seat. Knox grabs my wrist and jerks me back down roughly, digging his fingers into my flesh.

"You aren't going anywhere. This is all on you, Whisper." The growl that leaves his throat scares the shit out of me. I've never heard him like this. I swallow hard as groups of men shuffle into the room, taking up the seats that were left vacant minutes ago. I watch the way they all move, filing in like they are in for a big show.

"Is Steele fighting?" Knox looks away but when I turn to Callan, he nods.

"It isn't what you think."

"Is there anything you three can't do?" I ask teasingly but the tone in the room is dark. Something's not right. "What the hell is going on, Callan?"

"He lied, Whisper. We all fucking lied to our dad and Steele is taking the punishment for it. He made his decision," Callan says looking straight ahead. There's no emotion in his eyes which startles me. Callan has always been the nicer of the three, always smiling and playing but not now. He's hard as stone and his face a mask I can't read.

"What do you mean?" I ask, not sure if I really want the answer to that.

"You'll see," Knox says grinding his teeth. I watch and wait, hoping like hell that nothing bad is about to happen but I can feel it in the air. It's almost a slap in the face when I see a group of men walk out with shorts on and their hands taped. Is there more than one fight? Where is Steele? I glance around when I see him, rolling his shoulders and cracking his neck from side to side. My insides tremble when I see him stand on one side but no one else moves in that direction.

"Oh, my God," I gasp when it hits me. Knox grabs the back of my neck, dragging my face to his. He leans in closely so that no one else can listen to what he's about to say to me.

"You can't react. Not a fucking tear, not a sob. Do you understand me?"

"He can't fight them all, Knox. He'll be killed."

"He made his choice."

"Why was this his choice? What the hell could he be gaining from this?" I nearly squeal when he pulls me closer. His eyes stay locked with mine and his silent answer is all I needed. My insides drop, bile rising in my throat as he stares at me.

"Me. He's doing this because of me." Knox releases his hold on me before the man I recognize as their father steps into the ring.

"As you all very well know there was a job that my son was set out to do. Unfortunately, he took an interest in his job. When one of us disobeys orders, we have to be punished. That's the way the system here has always worked. These days are no different and just because he is my son doesn't give him a free pass. Now, there are still things of interest in this investigation but sad to say my boys will no longer be a part of it. From now on, all things go directly through me. This is what his decision was and I respect it. Now, sit back and take note. If anyone decides to disobey direct orders, you will find yourself inside this ring." The man walks out of the ring as Steele bounces on the balls of his feet. I can't watch this.

"What does that mean? This is how you deal with things?"

"When we disobey and don't follow his orders, this is the consequence," Callan says.

"Is that why I've seen him with bruises before?" I look over at him when he doesn't answer and watch as he swallows hard. Oh, my God. What kind of father is he to do this to his kids? No wonder they like to fight.

"Shut up and watch," Knox snarls.

"I can't watch this! What the hell is wrong with you, Knox?" I shove at his shoulder, but he doesn't move. Instead, he reaches for me, pulling me into his lap and pinning my arms down. I squirm, about to scream but he growls in my ear.

"They'll kill him if you leave."

"They'll kill him anyway! Look at them!" I hiss.

"I mean it, Whisper. You aren't going anywhere." The

finality in his tone should be enough to make me sit still but I can't. What if they kill him in that ring? What if he is doing this and dies anyway?

"Knox, please," I sob softly as he pulls me closer to him. He keeps me tightly in his embrace as the fight starts.

Each man takes a turn in the ring with Steele. The first few were fine, he held his own but now? Now they are getting worse. His eye is nearly swollen shut, blood drips down his face. My nails dig into Knox's arm as he keeps me close to him. My chest rises and falls as I watch the scene unfold in front of me.

"You can do this," I whisper as if he can hear me. I had it all planned out. I was going to make him pay for what he'd done to me. I was going to fuck with his head like he does mine but now all of that has shifted. I don't want to hurt him. I want to hold him. I want to kiss his soft lips and listen to the sound of his heart beat under my ear when I lay on his chest. I want him to hold me, tell me that everything is okay and that we will figure things out. I don't want to see him go down like this.

The crowd screams louder as my heart bangs a rhythm against my ribs. What have I gotten myself into with these men? It seems like hours go by when in fact, it has only been minutes. Steele hits the ground and I rise to my feet. I fight Knox off me and rush down the aisle and into the ring, dropping to my knees next to him. Wiping his hair away from his face, I nearly scream.

"Steele? Jesus, wake up, Steele."

"I'm not dead, Whisper. Stop fucking babying me." God, I've never been so happy to hear a smartass comment as I am right now. "You need to leave."

"What? No. I'm not going anywhere," I tell him as I wipe the blood from his lip. He lazily reaches up and grabs my wrist, holding it in his hand.

"You don't have a choice. Get up and walk out of here like you don't give a shit about me."

"Steele," I start to protest when his good eye opens and locks with mine.

"They will kill you, Whisper." His words slam into my chest as I fall back onto my ass. He watches me, shoving himself up on his elbows when Callan and Knox both drop next to us. Steele looks away from me and straight at Callan. They don't even have to speak. They just look at each other and know what the other wants. Callan nods and stands, coming around to lift me off the floor. I don't say a word as I let him lead me out of the ring and down the aisle. I look at faces, all the faces of the assholes that sat back and watched what they did to him. I make a mental note of every single one of them.

"What are you doing?" Callan asks when I stop to eye his dad up and down.

"Making a mental note of all the motherfuckers I'm going to kill."

20

STEELE

"Did you check on her?" I ask, holding my ribs as I reach for my bottle of water.

"Yeah. She's fine, Steele. She's pissed though," Callan tells me. I wish she didn't have to see that.

"She has heart; I'll give her that much." Callan shifts so that he's facing me.

"No, man. I don't think you understand. She looked at every single person in that room that night and said she was making a note of who she had to kill later." That sparks my interests. I glance over at my brother and shake my head.

"I don't think you really know what that girl is capable of, Steele." This time it's Knox that chimes in.

"She does. She knows who she is," I inform them. They both jerk their heads to look my way. I didn't want them in the middle of this shit with our dad. I didn't want them to take the fall for a decision I made.

"You didn't think to tell us? What the hell is with you, Steele?"

"I didn't want you in the middle of it. Either of you. I choose to keep her around, not you," I remind them both, pointing my bottle in their direction.

"If she knows then she knows about Nathan and Debra too," Callan adds.

"Yeah. I can't guarantee that won't end well for them," I chuckle.

"Are you listening to yourself? She isn't like us, Steele. She wasn't raised the way we were."

"Don't you think I know that? She might not have been raised here but she sure as hell is more like us than any of you realize. She's unstable, Knox! She's just as tormented and ruined as we are!" It's not a lie. We're all a little fucked in the head and Whisper isn't far behind. Just because she hasn't had to endure the abuse that we have doesn't mean she didn't endure her own kind of hell out there in the world. In fact, I know she did. I only heard a few stories from her, and I wouldn't wish that on anyone.

"Damn it. What are we going to do?" Callan asks.

"That's the thing. I don't know. Our plan was always to turn Dad and McLean against each other. Let them kill each other over this shit while we sit back and watch. Maybe we need to let that happen," I suggest.

"What about her?"

"What about her?" I snap in Callan's direction.

"She's a threat, Steele. To all of us. You know as well as I do that if she wants it all, she just needs to look a little further. All it will take for her to ruin us is one phone call. Did you ever think about that while you were drilling your cock in her?" That's enough of that shit. I leap off the couch, pain shooting through my body as I lunge at him. My fist collides with his cheek, his head snapping to the side. Knox is pulling me back in seconds, shoving us apart.

"We don't fight! We don't do this! Is she going to be a problem between us, Steele?"

"Only if he makes it one," I snarl nodding at my little brother.

"We all care about her, Steele. I get that but what happens when she wants more? Huh? You think any of us bastards giving a fuck about her will make a difference?" He has a point and I get it. Trust is something you earn and sadly she hasn't earned that from us. Whatever this is I feel for her doesn't matter when it comes to my brothers and that's the part I need to remember. We were one before her and we'll be one after her.

"You're right. We keep her close. We move on with our plans, but we make sure that McLean is out of the way first. Any proof of Whisper Jane Macron dies with him. Understood?" I look between my brothers as they both nod, the air calming around us. Callan is the first to walk away when Knox blows out a breath and drops into the chair across from me, resting his head in his hands.

"This is a mess," he says softly.

"Not really. I think we can keep her in check long enough to get what we want. If McLean and all the proof is gone, she has no say in anything." Knox looks up at me, his eyes holding questions.

"Are you going to be able to pull the fucking rug out from under her like that, Steele?"

"We're family, Knox. My family always comes above all else. Dad has fucked us over. He's made our lives a living hell and now it's our time to take over. It's our time to make the moves that we all know need to be made. Keeping things in Rolling Springs is holding this family back. Think about what we could be doing out there in the world? Overseas? It has to be this way, Knox."

"She means something to you, Steele. I can see it," he adds. I nod my head because I won't lie and say she doesn't. Even though I want to snap her neck for who she truly is, how can I blame her for being born? It's simple. I can't.

"You're right, she does. Just like she's grown on you and Callan but when it comes down to it, who would you choose?" His eyes flicker with fire before he nods his head.

"It's always been us three."

"And it still is." I don't know if I have the heart to completely ruin Whisper but if it comes down to her or my brothers, I won't be choosing her.

"You still hitting the masquerade ball?" I raise an eyebrow.

"It's two days away. You're damn right we're going." Knox laughs as I take another long pull from my water and fall back onto the soft pillows of the couch. Blowing out a breath, he stands and starts to walk away when he stops and turns back to look at me.

"For what it's worth, I wouldn't blame you for keeping her, Steele." I don't respond because frankly, I don't know what to say to that.

21

WHISPER

I can't feel my toes, or my hands for that matter. Nathan and Debra weren't here when I came home a few days ago, so I did what any pissed off eighteen-year-old would do. I stole all the liquor and got drunk. Pity party of one. I've drank until everything blurs and now I sit here... numb. I hated what happened to Steele, I hated it even more when Callan drove me back here and not to their house. Something in my chest pinched and it hurt like hell. Since I've been here, I've searched more. I know what I'm looking for and I have the number on speed dial now ready to use at my discretion. I almost dialed it yesterday. My real mom. The real woman that gave birth to me only to dump me off because I didn't have the right father. She should win an award, that bitch. Mother of the fucking year. I giggle at my own joke when the door opens.

"I'm afraid, Nathan," I hear Debra say. I roll my eyes.

"You should be!" I call out. The two of them close the door and come into the living room where I sit with their bottle of whiskey. Bringing it to my lips, I swallow another long pull.

"Is it not bad enough you're off fucking the Alder boys and now you're underage drinking." I smirk when Nathan speaks. Idiot. Lifting the gun that rests in my right hand, I wave at him and motion to the couch across from me.

"What the hell?" Debra nearly squeals.

"Sit the fuck down, Debra. Don't make me tell you twice," I say in the prissiest tone I can muster. God, I almost sounded just like her. Her and Nathan both move to sit and watch me. I take another drink. I don't want to be too drunk though, it is Halloween and all and I have a dance to get to.

"What's going on, Whisper? Did something happen?" Nathan asks as if he was a caring parent. I snort a laugh, whiskey shooting from my nose. With the same hand that holds the bottle, I bring it up and wipe it on the back of my hand.

"That was funny all things considered."

"What are you tal—"

"No! That's enough talking out of you two. It's my turn to ask the questions and it's your turn to give the answers." The smirk on Nathan's face makes me think that he thinks I'm joking. Maybe I should blow his balls off. Or cut his beating hands right from his no-good body.

"Do you know who I am?" I ask first, knowing they have to know by now. The whole goddamn town does.

"Whisper."

"Good one, Nathan! I think we're all aware of that fact. I mean do you know who I really am?" I hiss the words. They share a look that tells me they do.

"When did you find out?" Debra asks. Perfect Debra. Always so goddamn put together in her fancy blouses and pencil skirts. She makes me sick to even look at.

"Not long ago actually. It wasn't hard after I went searching and found my half-sister." Both of them raise their eyebrows.

How cute, neither of them knew about her. "It was a shock to learn that she was a year younger than me, but she, too, was dumped off to fend for herself. Ironic isn't it?" I look between them and take another drink. "Funny thing about that is, she isn't nearly as vindictive as I am. She lives here amongst all this trash and lies. She works in the very school she wasn't allowed to attend because of her bloodline." I laugh.

"What are you talking about?" Nathan snaps.

"Shut up, Nathan!"

"I will kill you," he growls as he begins to stand. I wave the gun around, a reminder that I'm in charge now. He sits back next to his horrid wife.

"I don't think you will. You were using me to get back into the good graces of the Alder's, weren't you?" Debra's face pales as she looks at me before quickly averting her eyes.

"Maybe. So what? Do you realize how much you're worth to Dennis Alder?" Ugh, just hearing his name makes my stomach roll. That bastard.

"Not enough, apparently. Didn't you hear that Steele took his punishment… for me?" The smirk that crosses my face must piss him off. His hands clench in front of him as I laugh.

"You're lying!"

"Am I?" I cock my head to the side as I raise the gun and aim. "I have no use for you two any longer. You used me, beat me and now it's time I repay the favor. You won't get what you want out of me. You won't be handing me over on a silver platter to dear old Daddy Alder because you won't be alive to see tomorrow." Pulling the trigger, I move the gun to Debra and do the same. I never thought about taking a life. It never really crossed my mind, but after all the pain that I've had to endure in my life, I think it was well deserved. Too bad the idiots didn't pay attention that it was their own gun and there won't be any fingerprints. I also love the fact that we are far enough away from neighbors that no one would have heard those two shots. The thing that makes me laugh about these two is how gullible they were. They thought they had a plan all along.

Dropping the gun on to the table, I stand up and walk over to Nathan. Reaching down, I run my gloved finger through the blood that seeps from his face and bring it to mine. I streak it across my face when I hear a horn outside. Looks like my ride is here.

I grab the mask that I bought for tonight and tie it around my face before looking down at my outfit. Shane told me that everyone dresses sexy as hell for the bash and so I did. In short leather shorts, a corset that I can barely breathe in and knee-high boots, I fit the bill the tonight. I grab the oversized sweatshirt that I stole from Steele and slip it on over my clothes before heading out the door, grabbing my backpack as I go. Strutting down the stairs and sidewalk, I climb in Shane's car.

"You are not wearing that shirt all night," she says pointing at me. I smile.

"Nope. I have to make an impression. You look hot," I tell her eyeing her up and down. She has on a pair of cut-off shorts that hug her frame and a crop top that looks to be two sizes too small but she rocks it.

"I plan on talking to Callan tonight," she says softly.

"No. None of that sad sounding shit. You are going to talk to him. Have some confidence, Shane." She nods her head, glares at me and narrows her eyes.

"Nice fake blood!" she adds before putting the car in drive and pulling out. I want to laugh but I don't. Instead, I shrug and watch out the window as she drives. It doesn't take us long to pull up in the Intensity parking lot. There are cars for miles and when we step out, I nearly curse the line. I start walking toward the back of the line when I see Callan. His eyes meet mine before shifting to Shane and back. He jerks his head so that we follow him. Glancing at Shane, she just shrugs. I'm sure they are all pissed at me for not showing up while Steele was recovering but I needed some time to adjust and get my head right. Besides, Callan is the one that drove me home. Not like I can go back there now.

We walk in behind Callan as he nods at the security guard. Shane wraps her arm around mine as we strut into the room. I see Leddy right away and toss her a small wave. Her eyes light up as she waves back. We've talked a few times since the first time I was here. She's actually really nice and asked me about going to school for dance. We talked for hours one night about it.

"You should have come by," Callan hollers above the music.

"I wasn't sure I was invited. I did get dropped off and all," I smart ass him. He nods his head when he looks past me. Something flickers in his eyes. It's the danger that lingers around Steele. I can feel him. Large hands clamp onto my hips, pulling me back into a hard body.

"Where the hell have you been?" he asks, leaning down so it vibrates through my ear.

"Handling business."

"You didn't even come check on your man?"

"My man?" I ask spinning to face him. His eyes stay locked on mine through the holes in the mask before slowly moving over the bloody streaks on my cheeks. For a second, I think he's going to ask me about them, but he doesn't.

"I like the hooker boots," he says, pulling back and avoiding his own question. I smirk and look to my left when I see Knox. Walking away from Steele, I head straight for his brother.

"Are we dancing tonight?" I ask him. He spins around, leaving the girl he was talking to, to face me. His eyes rake over me before I grab the hem of the sweatshirt and pull it up and off. Tossing it to Shane, she giggles while Knox eyes me again. A slow dark smile curls his lips as he takes me in. Then, he leans in closer.

"I know what real blood smells like, Whisper."

"That makes two of us, Knox. Now answer the question," I say.

"You want to rile up the devil on Halloween?" he asks tilting his head to study my face.

"What a better night to summon demons."

22

———

STEELE

igh-heeled knee-high boots that beg to be wrapped around my waist. Skin tight leather shorts that I'd like to shred into many little pieces hug her ass. And yet she's over there dancing with Knox. Is she trying to get a rise out of me? Is she trying to piss me off? It's working perfectly and the thought of hurting her drifts across my mind.

"Haven't seen you around lately." I almost tell the body that belongs to that voice to take a fucking walk but instead I use it to my advantage. You want to play, Whisper? Game fucking on. I turn to see Tricia standing next to me, bright red lips painted to perfection like always.

"Been dealing with a lot." I don't give her a chance to respond when I grab her and pull her into me. She gasps but I ignore it. The song is hot, beating through the speakers as everyone dances and has a good time. That's when I notice her looking. Whisper sees me now. Bet she didn't think I'd play this game with her. She wants me to chase her and I'm not that kind of man.

"Where have you been? I've missed you." Tricia moans as I run my lips over her shoulder. I don't answer her this time either. I move our bodies to the beat and keep my eyes on Whisper. She spins around, pressing her ass into Knox and reaching behind his head to grab onto his neck. His hand comes to rest low on her stomach. They know what they're doing. They want to test my patience and sadly for them I don't have much left.

"Steele," Tricia whines as my fingers find her nipple through the flimsy fabric she has on. I pinch and pluck, tug until she's panting and pushing into me. But that's when I see it. Whisper grabs Knox's hand, shoving it into her shorts. He tries to pull back, but she doesn't let him. I'm thirty seconds away from losing it and crushing my brother's skull.

"That hurts," Tricia says as I pull harder. Knox's eyes roll back.

Twenty.

His body presses closer to her.

Ten.

Her lips part.

Five.

She starts grinding against his hand.

One.

Just as I shove Tricia to the side and start toward them, Leddy grabs my arm and brings the mic to her mouth.

"How are we all doing tonight?" The crowd screams as I glance around, bodies blocking my view of them.

"Are we all ready for the dance off? Who is going to be our Devil and his Disciple tonight?" Once more, the crowd roars to life. Leddy is known for amazing parties and Halloween is one of her favorites. Slowly, the music starts to blend with a new song and everyone slowly parts in the middle. A girl in a devil costume leads her man out onto the floor and they begin to dance.

"Calm down lover boy. I already claimed Knox for the dance off," Leddy whispers in my ear. I shake my head and tug at my hair as we watch. They do their thing and then the music fades into a new one letting a new couple know it's their turn. Leddy passes the mic off to someone else before she pushes her spandex covered body through the crowd and right in the center. Knox comes out as if on cue and they begin their dance.

"Hey, Steele!" I look to my left and see Callan with Shane attached to his arm. It's about time those two talked shit out.

"Nice," I say nodding toward her.

"We're going out. Call you later," he hollers over the crowd. I nod my head and turn back to watch Leddy and Knox. The chemistry between the two is off the charts but Knox isn't anywhere near ready to be with just one girl. Hell, I didn't think I was either but now all that consumes my mind is Whisper and all the dirty things I want to do to her.

The music changes and Leddy and Knox leave the floor just as Whisper steps out there. Her body moves with ease as I part the crowd and make my way to the edge of it. I don't step into the middle, not yet. I want to see her. Watch her move. And she does move. Her body lowers to the floor before she spreads her legs into a split and raises back up. She pops her back, locks it in place before spinning with her arms above her head. She's magical. The motions so fluid and free. She drops to her knees when her eyes find mine. I step out into the open space and watch her as she crawls across the floor. With her gripping my thighs, I roll my hips, my hard cock pressing against her lips. She spreads her knees, dropping a little lower before climbing to her feet. I grab her hand, spinning her out and back in before gripping her hips like my life depends on it.

"I'm going to make you pay for letting my brother touch you." Before she can say anything further, I shove her away from me. I roll my hips, popping my back before spinning and watching her. Her eyes roam my body as she makes her way back to me. The music changes and I lift her in my arms carrying her out of the middle. The cheers don't stop as the next person takes our spot.

"You're a cock tease."

"You're an asshole."

"And yet you can't seem to stay off my cock," I add. I reach up and run my fingers over the dried blood that she didn't think I noticed when my phone buzzes in my pocket. I reach in and pull it out seeing it's Callan. He never calls unless something happens.

"What?" I snap into the phone, a little aggravated that he's interrupting me.

"We got a problem. Get Knox and meet me at the square." The line goes dead before I have the chance to ask what happened. Whisper watches me with wide eyes but I just shake my head, grab her hand, and drag her with me through the crowd. I find Knox with Leddy at the bar.

"We need to go. Something's up," I tell him. He nods and sets his drink on the bar before turning and pressing a kiss to Leddy's cheek. I lean in and do the same.

"I'm staying," Whisper protests, pulling her arm out of my grasp. I smirk.

"Like hell you are," I growl. I move toward her when Leddy stops me.

"Let her stay. I'll keep her company." I heard the tone in Callan's voice. Whatever it is, I know it's not good and I'm not leaving Whisper on her own at this point. I shove past Leddy and grab Whisper's arm once more, dragging her behind me.

She doesn't bitch and I'm happy for that. She needs to listen to me.

Once we're outside, Knox glances over at me but I just shrug because I have no idea what's happening.

"He said to meet him in the square." Knox nods and climbs in the driver's seat as I usher Whisper in the passenger side. She doesn't protest that either and it makes me wonder where that blood came from. No one speaks when I get in until I lean forward and wrap my hand around her throat.

"Is this little meeting about something you did?" I ask her. She turns her head as much as I'll allow it.

"Depends. What do you think I did?" There she is. The little shit that I knew lived inside of her. She's always been mouthy, and I like that but this? This is a spark of darkness that she doesn't let shine all the time.

"Well, I'm wondering where you got the blood on your face from. Care to share?" She grins, licks her lips and says, "Not a chance in hell."

I nod my head letting her have a minute, but this conversation is far from over. I will find out what the hell she did one way or another. Sirens sound in the distance and Whisper smiles to herself.

"What the hell is going on?" Knox mumbles to himself as he pushes the gas harder. We make it in a short time to the square and park. The square used to be the old town square, but McLean and his little followers decided that they needed a new one built on the other side of town. Now this is a meeting place of sorts. Knox pulls the car over to the curb and we all climb out. Callan sits on the bench with Shane tucked close to his side.

"This good?" I ask, nodding at her.

"Yeah, it's all good."

"What's going on?" Knox asks as we all come to a stop in front of him.

"The librarian from school was killed." Whisper gasps, her hand coming up to cover her mouth. I glance over at her but drag my gaze back to my brothers.

"What the hell does that have to do with us?" I ask annoyed that he pulled us from a damn good party for this shit. I don't care what happened to the librarian.

"It's our town, Steele."

"Probably her boyfriend," I grumble. His eyes move to Whisper and then it all hits me. The blood. Sirens. Did she kill her?

"You did this?" I roar, turning to face her. She scrunches her nose up and looks at me like I've grown two heads. "Is that where the blood came from?"

"Why the hell would I kill her?" Whisper snaps, getting in my face.

"Why the hell did you shove my brother's hand in your pants? I don't know why you do half the shit you do, Whisper!"

"It wasn't her!" Callan roars. We all turn to look at him confused.

"What? How do you know that?"

"Tell them, Whisper," he says softly bringing his eyes to meet hers. What the hell is going on?

"I don't know what you're talking about." Callan moves to stand, rushing at her and wrapping his hand around her throat. Her eyes widen as the rest of us watch. Callan isn't like this, this isn't him. I've never seen him lose control the way he is right now. He backs Whisper up, slamming her roughly against the brick of a nearby building.

"Tell them who she was." His teeth are grinding, his jaw locked tight.

"What the hell is this?" Knox asks, moving toward them. I raise my hand to stop him. I want to see how this plays out.

"Tell them!"

"Okay!"

"Now!"

"Okay! I didn't kill her!"

"Tell them why!"

"Fuck! I didn't kill her! She was my half-sister! Happy now?" Whisper screams in his face. I take a step back wondering exactly how any of them knew this and Knox and I didn't.

"Sister?"

"Yeah. She's the one that told me who I was. She knew." Her tone has quieted a lot as Callan releases the hold on her. I run my hand through my hair when it all hits me hard. If someone killed her sister for telling her, then they know who she is now.

"We have to go," I say mainly to myself.

"What?" That comes from Callan.

"They will come for her too."

"Who will?" Knox asks moving in next to me. I tug at my hair letting it all seep in. This is bad. This is really bad. There's only one person that can help us now. One person that I never wanted to be involved with.

"We need to go. Now!" I snap. I move toward Whisper and grab her arm, pulling her along with me. Shoving her roughly into the back of the car, I climb in the driver's seat and wait for the rest of them to get in before taking off.

23

WHISPER

I can still remember the beat of the very first song I danced to. It was hypnotizing. I remember letting my body just take over and do what it wanted. Even at a young age, others knew I could dance. They would invite me outside with them all the time. I think my foster parents hated the idea of it, but they were too out of it to actually tell me to stop. I wouldn't have anyway. I'm free when I dance. There are no chains around my heart, no shackles holding me in place. There's only me and the vibrations that work through my body. Those are memories that I will keep with me forever.

This car ride seems to be taking hours. Steele hasn't once looked in the rearview mirror at me as he drives. His eyes are locked straight ahead. Knox is in the passenger seat asleep and Shane has her head in Callan's lap snoring softly. This night has taken a toll on everyone. Mostly me. I never got to know her. I never got to see more of her and for some reason that hurts. I can't help but think about it and blame myself for Crystal's death. She told me. She shouldn't have but she did. I wonder if she knew that was a risk? That someone could have found out that she told me.

Shaking the thoughts away, I glance out the window. I don't know if I should mourn the loss of her or not. I didn't even know her, yet she did me a favor.

"Stop thinking." I look up and catch Steele's dark eyes on me, this time in the mirror.

"It's hard not to." He nods and looks back out the front window. Another ten minutes and we're pulling down a dirt road. All the thumping must wake everyone else up. They all shift and look around when Knox speaks.

"Haven't been here in a long time." Shane rubs her eyes before looking over and giving me a soft smile that I don't return.

"Figured it's the safest place until we figure this out," Steele adds. Callan grunts his agreement as I watch the small cabin come into view. It's nothing fancy like their house. It's almost... calming.

The car comes to a stop and everyone climbs out. I stretch and glance around at nothing but trees. The guys all move toward the cabin as Shane comes up to me.

"You okay?" I shrug. Am I?

"I don't really know. I'm sorry you got drug into this," I tell her, not knowing what else to say.

"Don't be. Come on." I let her lead the way and watch as she climbs the steps behind Callan. I don't make a move to go in until Steele comes back out. He stands in the doorway, his arms stretched over his head, hands resting on the doorframe.

"You going to stay outside all night?" I don't respond. Just stare up at him blinking. "Whose blood is it?" I shake my head.

"Is it Nathan's?" I can tell by the look in his eyes that he already knows the answer. Asshole.

"He was using me."

"To do what?"

"Get back into everyone's good graces. I don't know who he was delivering me to, but I know that was the plan." Steele's eyes darken as his arms fall to his sides.

"Come inside." I nod once and climb the steps, exhausted from the day. I thought I felt high as hell when I killed them but now all I feel is drained. I walk past Steele and into the cabin. I hear the others talking but I look up at Steele.

"Where's the bedroom?" He can see it, how worn out I am and I'm glad he doesn't act like a dick this time. Instead, he grabs my hand, weaving our fingers together as he leads me to a set of stairs. We descend into the basement when he reaches over and flips a switch. The lights come on revealing a bedroom. Looking at the plush blanket, I just want to crawl under it and never come out.

"Bathroom's in there. I'll leave you some clothes to put on," he says before releasing his hold on me. I don't know what I was expecting. Maybe I was waiting for him to be a little moodier than normal? Slam me around a little? I'm not exactly sure but being nice the way he is, wasn't it. Nevertheless, I walk into the bathroom and flip on the light. I sit on the toilet and unzip my boots, tossing them to the side before I stand and strip out of my clothes. I lost the mask in the car and now that I look at myself in the mirror, I feel sick. I killed them. I felt like a completely different person as I pulled the trigger.

"You're so stupid," I whisper to myself. How could I have done that? I killed someone. Bile rises in my throat and I'm hugging the toilet in no time. I guess when the alcohol wears off, you realize what you've done.

"You okay?" Steele's voice drifts through the bathroom as I heave once more.

"I killed them," I whisper. Steele curses under his breath before coming up behind me. He slides his arms under mine and lifts me from the floor before turning and starting the shower. I feel weak. I feel disgusting. I thought seeking vengeance would make me feel a little better and for a while it did. Steele releases me long enough to pull his clothes off before ushering me into the shower.

"What have I done?" I ask, looking up at him with confusion racing through me.

"You did what you had to do," he answers, reaching up and running his fingers along my cheek.

"I killed someone, Steele!"

"I know you did, baby." He called me baby. He's never called me that before. What's happening? What's happening to me? I feel like I'm slowly crumbling and there's nothing I can do to stop it. My heart's beating too quickly. I can't slow it. My mind is racing.

"What did I do?" I whisper as he pulls my head to his chest.

"Everything's okay, Whisper. I promise."

"You can't promise that! They killed her for talking to me, didn't they?" Lifting my head, I look into his eyes. Steele slowly nods his head before I lose it. Tears that I don't let flow easily spring to my eyes and fall down my cheeks.

"She's dead because of me." His hands move quickly, grabbing my face roughly.

"No. Not because of you! She's dead because you and she were secrets, Whisper. You weren't supposed to come back to Rolling Springs."

"Why did it have to be that way? We were babies, Steele. We didn't know any better!" Anger creeps in overriding the guilt. I ball my fists and slam them into his chest and he lets me.

"What could we have done? Huh? We were babies! We

didn't ask to be born." Hit after hit, he takes every one of them until my body just gives up. The high I was on, the alcohol induced bliss is gone and there is nothing left in me. My body goes limp and I fall into Steele's arms. He lowers us to the floor of the shower, just holding me in his arms. The blood that stained my cheeks is now leaking down his chest and I can't find it in me to move.

"I got you, Whisper." His words are a comfort and a curse. He can't have me. He can't keep me because that would go against all his father has built. It would against their fucked-up rules.

"Don't hate me when it's all over, Steele," I say as my eyes slowly begin to flutter closed. My chest aches.

"I could never hate you."

"You will." And as the new plan forms in my head, I know for a fact that he's going to hate me just as soon as I can figure all this out.

24

———

STEELE

She broke down last night. I put her in bed and watched her worn out body as she slept. Her words ring in my head and I can't make them stop, not even now as I watch her on the front deck, headphones in her ears as she dances freely.

"She okay?" Callan asks, taking a seat next to me.

"No."

"That's it? Just no?" He chuckles.

"She's messed up, Callan. She killed Nathan and Debra."

"Shit," he hisses under his breath. Shit is right.

"You talk to her?" I shake my head.

"She was a mess. Fell asleep."

"She looks okay today," he says, sounding as confused as I feel.

"Yeah, doesn't make any sense does it?" He looks over at me and I shrug.

"You think she's planning something." It isn't a question and if I can feel it, so can he. I nod my head once when she spins around and spots us watching her. A smile tugs across her face before she goes back to her dancing.

"You see that? Last night she was breaking down in tears. Shaking and not able to talk. Now she's dancing and smiling, Callan. Fucking smiling!" I growl.

"She's coping."

"No, it's more than that." I bring the cup of coffee to my lips and watch her a little more. She's up to something. I can feel it. But what? What does she know that I don't?

"What do you want to do?"

"Our plan needs to move faster than we planned on. Dad needs out. McLean needs handled."

"I agree but how are we going to get them all at once? By now they have to know about Nathan and Debra."

"They don't give a shit about them," I add.

"No, probably not, but who the hell were they delivering her to?" That's a damn good question. One I don't have an answer for. I lean back in my seat and take her in. The way she moves, her body flexing. It would be wrong to keep her. It would be wrong to want to claim her and give her the goddamn world. So why do I want to do just that?

"Can I do anything?" Shane's voice sounds behind us. Callan turns, looking over his shoulder with a smile. He nods for her to come to him and she does.

"We're just thinking. You okay?" he asks her. I know he's missed her. Shit went down with our dad years ago. Shane got stuck in the middle and the fact that she was basically a nobody had Callan choosing sides. My dad told him that if he didn't want her to suffer, he would walk away. He did just that and it broke the man in the process.

"Dad," I say softly.

"What?"

"Dad. Who the hell else would stand to lose anything? Her mom's dead. Has been for years."

"And her dad? Where the hell is Macron?" That's the question isn't it. Where he is?

"We need to go see Andy."

"McLean? Why?" Callan asks.

"Think about it. Dad has kept tabs on him for years. Why? Why does he care what that asshole does? We have far more power than he does."

"Jesus Christ," Callan mumbles. It all must hit him at once. I smell the weed before Knox comes strolling in with a joint between his lips.

"What are we talking about?" he asks, passing me the joint. I take it in my fingers and bring it to my lips, inhaling deeply.

"We just figured out who Whisper's dad is," I inform him. He looks at me and furrows his brows.

"Who?"

"Andy McLean."

"Bullshit," he says with a half smirk.

"Think about it. Dad keeps Andy close, right? Why? Why would he do that? The Alder's run it all. The only one that could possibly challenge that is that little dancer out there on the porch." All eyes turn to her. She must feel it because she stops dancing and slowly turns to face us all. Her eyes bounce from one person to the next before they stop on mine. I motion for her to come inside and I'm almost shocked when she does.

"What the hell are you all staring at?"

"We think we know who your real dad is," I inform her.

"What? Who?"

"Andy McLean." She shakes her head slowly, her lips parting. "What? What is it?"

"A. M."

"What?"

"A. M…" she shakes her head. "I've had a phone number. It was given to me so long ago. I…"

"What number, Whisper? What are you talking about?"

"A number! The initials on the paper were A. M. I was told that if I ever got into too much trouble to call the number! I never called it. I never thought about it. I just saved it in my phone and that was it. I didn't need any help. I've never needed help!" I shove out of my chair and grab her shoulders, forcing her to calm down and focus on me.

"Whisper. It could be a trap. I need to know that number." She shakes her head, looking confused, but pulls her phone from her pocket. She passes it to me, and I tap the screen pulling up her contacts. A. M. is right there at the top. I almost lose it when I open it and see the number attached.

"You have got to be shitting me!" I roar, squeezing the phone in my hand so hard I'm afraid it may snap.

"What? Who is it?" Knox moves to stand closer to me. Shock is a bitch. I can feel it in my chest. The phone is taken from my hands.

"It's Ray. It's Ray's number," Knox says.

"No way. What the hell does Ray have to do with any of this?" Callan roars as he jumps to his feet. It's all too damn much. I've trusted Ray. He's been more of a father to me than my own has.

"Steele?" Whisper says my name, but I can't deal with her right now. "Steele?" One more time and I snap. I drag my heated gaze toward her, anger and rage coursing through my veins.

Grabbing her around the back of the neck, I slam her body against the wall.

"Stop saying my name!"

"Steele!" Knox roars.

"You are fucking up everything! Maybe I should be the one to hand you over, huh? Pass you off to Dad so he can kill you as planned?"

"Steele!" This time it's Callan.

"Do your best, Steele. You think I haven't been broken before?"

"Not by me." She laughs. Laughs in my face.

"You aren't the worst of the worst, Steele. You think you are. I've brushed myself off every single time and you know what? I've picked up the pieces and glued them together all by myself." Why does that piss me off more?

"The problem with me? I will take those pieces, Whisper. I'll take them and you will never get them back," I growl in her face.

"That's enough, Steele!" Callan's hands come down on my shoulders jerking me away from Whisper. I watch the fire, that spark in her eyes as it ignites. She wants to push me, and God help me I want her to. Instead, I turn on my heel and storm toward the basement door.

"Don't you walk away from me!" I stop dead in my tracks when I hear her voice. Slowly, I turn to face her. The look in her eyes, God, why does she affect me like this?

"I already did." She tilts her head to the side to study me a second.

"So that's it? You walk away from me?"

"What are we, Whisper?" She looks at me confused.

"What do you mean?"

"I mean, what the hell are we? Boyfriend, girlfriend? Fuck buddies? What?" That's a low blow even for me.

"We aren't shit, Steele." She turns this time to walk away and I feel like a complete asshole. Not that I will try to stop her. I won't. I need the space to breathe. I need to make sure that she's far enough away from me when this ticking time bomb inside of me blows, because once it starts, there will be no stopping me.

25

———

WHISPER

Steele won't even look in my direction and on one hand, that stings. But on the other hand, it's better this way. We were testing each other's patience from the day we met. Neither of us were willing to back down from the showdown that is us.

"He'll come around," Callan says, resting his hand on top of mine.

"I don't need him to. I need this to be over so I can get on with my life."

"I heard Leddy offered you a job. That's pretty awesome, Whisper." His smile is infectious, and I find myself smiling along with him.

"Yeah. I couldn't believe it. She talked with some of her people and they are opening a studio right outside of Rolling Springs."

"I'm proud of you. You know that right?" Why does he do this? Does he want me to cry? I'm not that girl. I don't cry over little things like this.

"Stop, Callan."

"No, I mean it. You deserve to be happy, Whisper. You deserve to have a life that you've always wanted and dancing is what you do. I'm really proud of you for not giving up," he quips.

"I will never give up. That's something I don't have in me. There were times I thought about it, but something would nag at me and I would just get back up and do it again." Callan smiles before pulling me into a hug. I don't know how I feel about this newfound friendship. I think I liked it better when he was a dick.

"You are one of the strongest people I've ever met. I have no doubt about anything you want to do, Whisper."

"Stop trying to make me cry, Callan!" I shove him back a step and he laughs as Knox walks up.

"What are you two fighting about?" He eyes me up and down like he always does with his heated gaze.

"She's going to work with Leddy at the new studio." Knox's eyes light up.

"No shit? Guess that means we will be seeing more of each other," he says making it a point to wiggle his eyebrows.

"What the hell does that mean?"

"Who do you think she asked to help?" I groan and roll my eyes even though I'm happy that Knox will be around when this is all over.

"God, kill me now."

"I can arrange that." Steele's growl vibrates through my body. Even when he's being a prick, I can't find it in myself to hate the man. In fact, it's almost the opposite. I want his brooding mean ass even more.

"You could try," I add.

"Is that a challenge?" He steps up behind me, his warmth

spreading through me like wildfire. His hand slowly wraps around my neck as he squeezes lightly.

"What are you doing, Steele?" I ask when he presses himself closer to me. I wish he didn't affect me like this. I wish I could walk away but I can't. He holds me in a cage that's surrounded by him. No matter which way I look, he's all I see.

"I think I'm claiming you right the fuck now."

"Claiming me?" I huff out a laugh. "I told you once, I don't belong to anyone."

"Yeah, I remember that but I also remember not giving a shit." I spin in his hold and look up into his dark eyes. If anyone were to claim me, I'd want it to be Steele.

"I don't like your attitude."

"I don't like your smartass mouth."

"I don't like how demanding you are."

"I don't give a fuck. I said you were mine and that's the end of the discussion."

"I hate you," I snarl, meaning it to a point. I do hate the way he causes me to react to him. I hate the way my body betrays me when we're close. There are so many things I hate about this man.

"I hate you too. Now shut the hell up and go sit down. We need to figure out what we're doing." I roll my eyes and pull out of his grasp before sitting on the couch next to Callan, throwing my leg over his. I make it a point to watch Steele squirm before winking at Shane. She knows what I'm doing.

"What are we doing?" Knox asks sitting on the other side of me, wrapping his arms around my waist. His fingers move slowly over my stomach as butterflies erupt inside of me. I like Knox and he can illicit feelings in me, but nowhere near what I feel for Steele. Nevertheless, I see the way Steele's jaw is clenching.

"First, you're going to get your goddamn hands off her," Steele growls. Knox laughs.

"I don't think so. She likes it when I touch her." I have to suppress the laugh that wants to escape me, biting my lips between my teeth. I can see Steele basically vibrating from here.

"We don't need to discuss anything. I already have a plan," I announce.

"Which is?" Steele asks dragging his eyes to meet mine.

"You're going to turn me in to your dad."

"Like fuck!" Callan roars, shoving my leg off his lap and standing to his feet.

"He's right, that's not smart, Whisper," Knox whispers in my ear. Callan paces the floor pulling at his hair before turning to Steele.

"Are you going to say something to her? Stop her?" He just shrugs and watches me.

"I think she's right. Turn her in."

"What the hell is wrong with you?" Callan snaps, moving in on him. I don't move and neither does Knox. We both sit here and watch what's happening because frankly, there is no way to stop them once they start.

"Should we help?" Shane asks.

"No," Knox and I say in unison. I grin at him over my shoulder.

"She could be killed!" Callan roars as Steele climbs to his feet.

"Yeah, she could." I snort a laugh.

"And you're okay with that? Huh, Steele?"

"No, I never said I was okay with it. I just simply said that she could. I just claimed her ass as mine, do you really think that I'd let him hurt her?" Steele's voice has changed. It's calmed as he talks to him now. I'm not sure how I feel about it to be honest. I get a tingly feeling at the way he says that he claimed me.

"Then what the hell are we doing?" Callan asks exasperated. He runs his hand through his hair and takes a step back from Steele. Shane stands and moves toward him, wrapping her arms around his waist.

"Five dollars says they already fucked," I say over my shoulder to Knox. He chuckles.

"Not a chance. I already know they did." We both laugh when Steele's eyes come to rest on us. "Stop laughing, we're stirring the beast." I giggle and lean my head back on his shoulder.

"Not like we haven't done that before."

"It won't happen again!" Steele's voice thunders through the room.

"Oh, it will happen again. Knox is a good dancer. I plan on taking him to Intensity with me when this shit's over." The way Steele's chest heaves, I know I need to stop, but that feral look in his eyes is one that I crave from him. Knox nudges me and slips off the couch, heading for the kitchen. I shove myself up off the couch and start to follow him when Steele's arms wrap around me. He lifts me off the ground and carries me to the steps, taking two at a time as he descends into the basement.

"What are you doing?"

"Giving you a goddamn reminder not to fuck with my head anymore."

26

STEELE

I t all feels like a bad idea. We've gone over it time and time again, but I still don't like it. I bring the joint to my lips and inhale deeply before blowing it through my nose.

"It feels wrong," I say once more.

"You've said that already." Callan the jackass says. It's not his girl that's going to be in the line of fire, it's mine.

"I know what you're thinking asshole and she means something to all of us," Knox chimes in, looking me dead in the eye. I hate that they can read me, but they are my brothers and we've always been close.

"Does she?" I ask, tilting my head to the side to look at him. I can see the fury in his eyes with that question. The truth is, I know how much she means to all of us and that pisses me off. I don't know exactly why but it does.

"Fuck you, Steele. I don't want anything to happen to her either!" Knox roars, clenching his hands at his sides. I straighten my spine ready to throw blows when she walks out of the cabin.

"What's with the pissing match?" she asks looking from Knox to me.

"Your man thinks he's the only one that can care about you," Knox tells her. Whisper laughs.

"Steele doesn't care about me. He cares about what he gets from me." That's it. I'm sick of this shit. I might not be big on feelings and all that, but I do know what I feel for her. Grabbing her shoulder, I spin her around to face me.

"Say it again and I will spank your ass raw." Whisper raises her eyebrows, her challenge waiting.

"Was it a lie?" she asks, placing her hands on her hips. I stick the joint back between my lips and inhale deeply. Holding the smoke in my lungs, I lean down into her face.

"Everything you just said was a lie," I say, blowing the smoke into her face.

"Are we sharing feelings now, Steele? Is that what you want to do?" I know she has a hard time with what she feels just as much as I do. I know she wants to deny it all and keep up that front, but I'll be damned if I let her downplay what we have between us.

"Yeah. I think it's about time shit gets out in the open, don't you?" There it is. The fire I've grown to love.

"Fine. You want truth? Here it goes!" She screams throwing her arms out wide.

"This is going to get good," Knox mumbles and Callan and Shane shift in their seats. I stand here with my arms crossed over my chest waiting.

"Let's hear it!" She turns to face me, her eyes full of fury.

"I've never been in a place where someone has actually cared about me. What I was, what I am is a pawn. My whole life has been one lie after another, and you can't stand here and tell me that the three of you didn't use me to your advantage!" And the bomb drops. So does my stomach. She stands with her eyes burning into me. So much anger still resides inside of her. So much hurt.

"Go ahead, Steele. Tell me that isn't true." I toss the joint to the ground, snuffing it out with the toe of my shoe before looking back up at her.

"You're right. You were a job that we were supposed to get close to. We were supposed to find out what you knew about your real parents. Then we were supposed to kill you." The small gasp that leaves her mouth tears my soul apart. She didn't know that part. I didn't want her to know that part. Slowly she looks to Callan and then Knox before hardening that shell of hers and looking back to me.

"Then why didn't you do it?" I shake my head, not sure how to explain this to her. She steps closer to me, sticking her hand in my pocket and before I can think about it, she has my switch-blade, flipping it open. "Remember the first time you used this on me?" Her voice is flat, not one single emotion coming through as she raises it to her throat. Her head slowly rises, and her eyes burn into mine.

"What are you trying to prove here?" I ask crossing my arms over my chest.

"That I'm disposable. Just like I've always been."

"Whisper. Please stop," Shane cries. Callan grabs her when she tries to stand up and pulls her back. He whispers in her ear, calming her a little.

"No one has wanted me alive. I don't know what's taken so long to do it. What are they waiting for? What are you waiting for?" she asks, staring me down. I see the slight tremble in her hand but when I don't answer, she presses the blade into her skin a little more. She never winces, just holds it there.

"What are you waiting for?" I ask her the same question she

asked me. Her eyes narrow slightly before she smirks. It's dark and haunted. Not one I want to see on her perfect face. Just as she's about to slit her throat, I move. I grab the knife in one hand, tossing it to the side and jerk her body against mine with the other.

"You forgot to let me finish," I growl. Whisper laughs darkly, shoving me away from her.

"By all means," she says, gesturing toward me while trickles of blood run down her neck.

"I thought about killing you at first. It made sense to just get it over with. I didn't really understand why my dad wanted you alive or to find out what you knew. Who gives a shit what you know, right?" She crosses her arms over her chest now, glaring back at me.

"Then things changed. Then I didn't really want to kill you. I wanted to keep you. Did Knox tell you why my dad had my ass beat that night?" She looks to Knox then back to me.

"Because of me."

"It wasn't just because I was fucking you, Whisper. It ran deeper than that. He pulled my rank in this family. He pulled my place and all that I worked for because I chose you! I chose you over my dad!" Shock registers on her face but I'm not done yet. Stepping closer to her, her arms fall to her sides.

"You are so stupid. So stupid, Steele! Why the hell would you give up your life for me?" She's mad. You have got to be kidding me.

"Are you kidding me right now? You have the balls to be pissed off when I just told you I gave up everything, I could have been killed, for you! You, Whisper!" She slams her palms into my chest shoving me back a step. Then another.

"You're so stupid! What the hell were you thinking?" Another shove.

"What was I thinking? I was thinking I wanted you more than that life," I roar.

"And you could have been killed, you idiot!"

"So what?"

"So what? Are you serious right now? Look around you, Steele! Your brothers need you! They are your family. Can you ever think about anyone but yourself?" Wow, she's really going there.

"I thought I was! I was thinking about you, Whisper." She shakes her head, running both her hands through her hair as she steps backward.

"No. No you…"

"Love you."

"What?" she asks, looking confused.

"I love you."

"Holy shit," Callan says under his breath.

"Saw that one coming," Knox adds.

"You don't. You don't love me. You love the idea of hurting your dad, of getting what you want." She isn't even making sense right now. I take the few steps between us, grabbing her face in my hands.

"Look at me."

"Steele, I can't."

"Look at me," I say in a gruff tone. Whisper slowly raises her eyes to meet mine and there I see them. The tears, the fears. She's never been loved before. Probably doesn't know what it feels like.

"I love you, Whisper. I love you. Not the idea of you, or of hurting him. You. Do you understand me?" Tears slowly fall down her cheeks as she swallows hard.

"I don't know what to say to you."

"Nothing. I don't want you to say anything. I know this is

new to you. I know you don't understand any of this but just know that I love you. Okay?" Whisper doesn't nod her head or say anything else. Instead, she rests her head on my chest as I wrap her in my arms.

"Well I think that went well." I roll my eyes at Knox, but he just laughs.

27

WHISPER

"You don't have to do this at all," Steele reminds me for the hundredth time. I don't have any other options. We don't have any other options. We have to go through with this.

"You said it yourself. This is the only way to get them all in one place. Just make sure you know what you're doing," I remind him. He hated the idea of coming back to Rolling Springs. He hated that I made that phone call too, but at this point, this is the only option we have. I grab his hand and drag him through the crowd of bodies. If we're going to take on his dad along with the others, I need one night of feeling free before we do. My dad, my real dad is set to be here in a few hours and before that confrontation takes place I need to breathe.

The music blasts through the speakers seeping into my bones. I watch Steele as his tense frame stands in front of me not wanting to be here. He didn't want me around Rolling Springs at all but here I am. I need to deal with this in my own way as much as he wants to deal with it in his. This is just my wind down.

I swirl my hips and smile as he stands like a statue. A damn nice-looking statue at that. Grabbing his hips, I try to get him to loosen up but he doesn't. When I've had enough, I lean in close to him.

"If you don't dance with me, I will find someone that will," I warn him. I turn my head and eye Knox when Steele's fingers come up and roughly grab my cheeks. He forces my gaze back to his.

"If you so much as look at him like that again, I will snap his neck." I grin.

"Then dance with me. I need this, Steele." He nods his head, waves his hand at someone and before I know what's happening all the music stops. I'm confused as hell but then a slow song comes over the speakers. I glance up at Steele as he pulls me closer to his body. He starts moving and everyone just parts for us. I don't know what this feeling is that washes over me but it's perfection. He holds me close, his breath dancing over the top of my head. I keep my face nuzzled into his neck as he moves us around the floor. I'm not much on slow dancing but being here in Steele's arms just feels right.

"Not everything has to be fast paced," he whispers. I look up and catch his eyes on mine.

"I'm not used to this," I inform him.

"I know that. That's why I'm not in a hurry to hear the words back, Whisper. I just needed you to know what I feel for you." Could he be any more perfect? When I first met Steele, I knew he was gorgeous, obviously, but there was more to him. I could see that spark inside of him and I wanted to reach out and grab it. The more I've gotten to know him the more I see and I like it. I can't say love because I'm not sure what that is.

"Thank you," I say softly. Steele leans down, pressing his lips to mine. I sigh at how content I feel in his arms. I don't think I've ever felt like this before. The music keeps playing but I can't hear the sounds. All there is, is him.

It doesn't take long for our moment to be broken by the phone vibrating in my pocket. I pull back and I slide it out to answer it.

"Hello?"

"You requested to see me. I'm here, at the square."

"I'm on my way." I hang the phone up and slip it back in my pocket before looking up at Steele.

"You sure about this?" he asks once more. I nod my head knowing what needs to be done. "You're going to own this world now."

"I told you to stop saying that. I don't want this world. I just want to dance, Steele."

"I know and you will but everything they have is about to be yours, Whisper."

"Ours. It's ours. I don't want any of this without you guys." Steele smiles and my heart leaps. I couldn't take his world from him. It isn't mine and even if it were, I wouldn't know what to do with it. Wrapping his hand around the back of my neck like he always does, he pulls me in and kisses my forehead.

"Let's go kill some parents." I laugh at the way he says it. Threading his fingers with mine, he leads me toward the door with Callan, Shane, and Knox right behind us. We all pile into the SUV as Callan drives toward the square. My stomach cramps as I think about meeting the man that didn't want me all those years ago. The man that gave me up. It's a hard pill to swallow, knowing someone didn't want you when you weren't even born yet.

"What are you thinking?" Knox asks, grabbing my other hand in his and squeezing.

"I just wonder what I'm going to feel once I see him."

"Don't force yourself to feel anything, Whisper. If it isn't there, it just isn't." I nod my head and squeeze his hand back before resting my head on Steele's shoulder.

"He's right. You can't force things, Whisper."

"I know. I'm not going to." The rest of the ride is silent. The silence gives me a chance to sort through what I feel which I'm still unsure of.

"Since we're all sharing feelings and shit this week, I just wanted to say that I love you too, Whisper," Knox blurts out.

"Fuck off, all of you," I laugh.

"Love you too, Whisper!" Callan calls over the seat. I laugh and curl into Steele, absorbing his warmth. I'm not sure what's about to happen and I'm not sure how I'm going to feel when it's over but for now I can enjoy just being here with him.

I close my eyes just as the car comes to a stop. I lift my head and look out the window taking a deep breath.

"You don't have to do this," Steele reminds me.

"Yes, I do." He nods and kisses me once more before climbing out. I follow him with the others not far behind. A man climbs out of another car, adjusting his jacket as he does. I gasp and stop in my tracks. My heart is beating so rapidly that I might pass out. No. I need this closure. I need this to end.

"Whisper?" he says when he looks up. I open my mouth but what can I say? It's him. It's my dad. My real dad. "It's nice to see you. I assume you're the Alder boys?"

"We are. I'd say it's a pleasure to meet you but it's not," Steele growls.

"I can understand that. Why is it you called me here? I assume it wasn't a reunion." He's straight to the point but I can't stop looking at him. He's real. A real person.

"I just needed to see you one time," I finally say, pulling myself together.

"I'm sure you have many questions," he adds as I shake my head.

"I actually don't. For the last eighteen years I've wondered what I did that was so bad that my own family didn't want me, but now? Now I just don't care. You're the reason I was broken. You're the reason my sister's dead."

"That was unfortunate."

"You knew?" I ask cocking my head to the side.

"Knew? Whisper, I'm the one that had her killed."

"What?" I start to lunge at him when Steele pulls me back.

"She wasn't useful to me. Neither are you," he adds, nodding toward me. I'm so confused. I don't understand.

"Neither are those boys. They chose their sides." We all stand still when we hear him speak. Steele looks to the left quickly, just in time to see his dad stepping out from behind the trees.

"What the hell is this?" Steele asks looking between them. That's when another man steps out. Ray? The coach?

"Hello, Whisper."

"Ray?" Knox moves closer to look at him. I hear Callan cursing behind us, but I can't stop looking at them.

"It was you," I whisper staring at him. Images flash behind my eyes. Flashbacks shake my body, but I can see him. "You didn't stop them," I say hoarsely. My throat feels like it's closing up. I can't breathe as I grab onto Steele's shirt and hold on like it's my lifeline.

"What the hell is going on?" Steele gets louder this time as he keeps one hand on me.

"Raymond Macron." The name slips past my lips as I remember him.

"What?"

"Our coach?" Knox asks looking confused.

"Well, I see that she is remembering things," Ray says

looking toward Alder. My stomach cramps as I think about it all.

"You're my dad. Raymond Macron."

"That can't be right," Callan says stepping closer.

"It's right son. For the last few years, I've set you boys up to take over this family. I've had plans of my own to move upward and onward. This could have been yours if you would have just handled the job you were given!"

"To kill her?" Knox asks, pointing to me. I watch the scene unfold but I don't let go of Steele. I can't.

"Exactly."

"What are they doing here then? You always said you hated them?" Steele asks. The men all chuckle like it's some big secret.

"Hate is a strong word, Steele. None of us were willing to kill children. That just went against all that we knew."

"What?"

"Whisper was a child. We weren't going to kill a child, so we watched her. Then one day, she got lost in the foster system. She was moved around so many times that we couldn't keep up. Apparently, Nathan and Debra found her. They thought using her to get back in with us would work. We let them think that. They were always going to die, it was just a matter of time. Until someone got to them first," McLean says.

"What about us? How the hell did we play into this?" Knox asks. I feel sick.

"You were supposed to go on about your business. Handle her and move on. All of this could have been yours until that night. I saw how you all looked at her. I knew it was over."

"Meaning what? You're going to kill us all?" Steele laughs but no one else does. Oh, my God. That was their plan. They were going to kill them. I slip my hand into Steele's pocket, wrapping my fingers around the switchblade. When everything goes silent in my head, I move.

EPILOGUE

Steele

"No, not there. Put that in the other room," I order the movers that are bringing in the dance equipment. It's been a year since everything's gone down. A year that we killed them all. A year that we've taken over.

"You are getting pretty bossy," Knox says with a smirk. Leddy elbows him in the ribs before he rubs it and smiles at her.

"I think it looks amazing. I can't thank you enough for helping with this, Steele. I mean, we had planned on doing this outside of Rolling Springs anyway but this? It's just amazing." I nod my head at Leddy before she leaps into my arms, hugging me. I knew she wanted a dance studio, but I also knew that I wanted to keep her close. It wasn't just about me anymore. It was about all of us. Leddy was there when we needed her, and she's always been a good friend. I decided that Alder Academy needed another dance space. One that offers classes that used to be available for students only. Leddy has always wanted to teach and why not let her?

"It's not a big deal. Make me proud though." She smiles and pulls back when Shane comes traipsing in.

"The sign is hung. Not like Callan helped though. The asshole left me standing on the ladder."

"I did not!"

"Lies, Callan!"

"Fine, I was watching your ass as you climbed up there. In my defense, if you weren't working here you wouldn't need to wear those damn leggings." We all laugh at him but he isn't wrong.

"You two are disgusting." Knox's turn to chime in.

"Yeah, like you haven't been looking at Leddy's ass all fucking day, man. Get out of here with that shit," I remind him, tossing the clipboard to the side. I stroll over and slap my brothers on the shoulder before strolling down the hall.

"Where are you going? She has a class!" Leddy yells behind me. I flip her off and keep walking until I get to the last room in the hall. I wait outside the door until all the kids come rushing out. I pull my phone out and connect to the speaker system in the room before heading inside and grabbing a chair. Sitting it in the middle of the floor, I wait for the music to play and Whisper to come back into the main room.

"We're done for today!" I hear her call out. She's been teaching a class to underprivileged kids. I knew she wanted to do that, give back somehow and this was just the place to do it. We started a program and I was amazed at just how many signed up. This town is changing and it's all because of her. She's made such a difference in a short amount of time that it amazes me. She amazes me.

"I said…" she cuts herself off when she sees me leaning back in the chair, my legs spread wide.

"What? What did you say?"

"What are you doing?" she asks playfully as she walks toward me. I don't say another word as she straddles my lap, her body pressing into mine. I run my hands up her sides and feel her squirm.

"I think they're playing your song," I whisper against her lips.

"Are they?" She kisses me and my whole world falls into place.

"They are. Dance for me, Whisper." She slowly slides off my lap and stands in front of me. The bass hits and so do her hips. I love watching her dance, but hip-hop is her thing. The way she can feel the beat and move her body with it. It's like nothing I've ever seen before.

Whisper moves with the music, sliding across the floor before leaping back to her feet. Swinging her hips, she spins and bends over, giving me a view of her ass. I groan and reach down to adjust my cock. She catches me and smiles, shaking her head.

"You remember that you crawled to me?" I ask her. She nods and stops moving.

"Is that what you're waiting for?" I nod my head once and watch as she dances a little more before dropping to her knees. She crawls across the floor like a sexual goddess until she's right in front of me. When I can't take anymore, I reach down and jerk her up into my lap. Crashing my mouth to hers, I take what I can get from her.

"I love you," I whisper against her lips.

"Fuck off, Steele."

"Say it," I growl biting into her lip.

"I love you too." She smiles happily before climbing off my lap causing me to groan.

"Where are you going?"

"Oh, it's your turn."

"For what?" She pulls me out of the chair before sitting in it and crossing her legs.

"Dance for me." She has no idea how much I would dance for her for the rest of my goddamn life.

"You only get one."

"Why only one?" She asks.

"Because we already agreed that you're going to be dancing for me for the rest of your life."

The End.

AFTERWORD

Did you enjoy Dance For Me? Consider leaving a review and if you think you can handle more of the Alder brothers, get Callan's story here: Stay With Me Alder Academy Book 2

Connect with Erin and find more of her hot romance books!
Connect with Erin! She loves her stalkers.
Newsletter:
http://bit.ly/ErinTrejoNewsletter
BookBub:
https://www.bookbub.com/authors/erin-trejo
Facebook:
https://www.facebook.com/authorerintrejo/
Facebook Readers Group –Fire and Ice
https://www.facebook.com/groups/1177887305577544/
Amazon:
https://www.amazon.com/Erin-Trejo/e/B00U0RXH80/
Twitter:

https://twitter.com/trejo_erin

IG:

https://www.instagram.com/authorerintrejo/